October, 1995

To Peter and Dotty -

With love and
Thanks for your wonderful
friendship and warm
hospitality. a bientot.

Miriam

A Place in the World Called
PARIS

EDITED BY
Steven Barclay

ILLUSTRATED BY
Miles Hyman

foreword by Susan Sontag

CHRONICLE BOOKS

SAN FRANCISCO

Pages 153–161 constitute a continuation of the copyright page.

Grateful acknowledgment is made for permission to reprint copyrighted material. Every reasonable effort has been made to trace the ownership of all copyrighted material included in this volume. Any errors that may have occurred are inadvertent and will be corrected in subsequent editions, provided notification is sent to the publisher.

To maintain the authentic style of each writer included in *A Place in the World Called Paris*, quirks of spelling and grammar remain unchanged from their original state.

Printed in Singapore.

ISBN 0-8118-0586-7

Library of Congress Cataloging-in-Publication Data available.

Cover illustration: Miles Hyman

Distributed in Canada by Raincoast Books,
8680 Cambie Street, Vancouver, B.C. v6p 6m9

10 9 8 7 6 5 4 3 2 1

Chronicle Books
275 Fifth Street
San Francisco, CA 94103

for Anne Lamott

ACKNOWLEDGMENTS

FOR THEIR ENCOURAGEMENT, generosity, and faith, I would like to thank William Abrahams, Susan Sontag, Gregory Riley, Marguerite Finney, Sydney Goldstein, Richard Overstreet, Odile Hellier of the Village Voice Bookshop, Frish Brandt, Fran Kiernan, Paul Auster, Stuart Bradford, Emily Broom, Alev Croutier, Mavis Gallant, Jane Hirshfield, Michael Katz, Andrew Harvey, Frances Mayes, Stefanie Marlis, Connie Matthiessen, Eliot and Margot Holtzman, Chula Reynolds, Agnès Montenay, Barbara Shulgasser, Sara Slavin, Mark Steisel, Mark Fox, Judith Moore, Jenny McDonald, Bill Hayes, Martha Jackson, Amanda Doenitz, Nicole Courtet, Leslie Graham, Peter McMillan and Gary Johnson of the Odyssey Bookshop, and the entire staff of A Clean Well-Lighted Place for Books.

There is, mother, a place in the world called Paris. A very
big place and far off and once again big.

César Vallejo

To know Paris is to know a great deal.

Henry Miller

Table of Contents

Preface by Steven Barclay   xv
Foreword by Susan Sontag   xvii

Conditions of Its Greatness   1

    Czeslaw Milosz
    Herbert Adams Gibbons
    John Berger
    Anaïs Nin
    Thomas Mann
    Walter Benjamin
    Grieben's Guide Book
    John Clellon Holmes
    T. S. Eliot
    Paul Auster
    James Weldon Johnson
    Gordon Parks

Place   11

    V. S. Pritchett
    Rainer Maria Rilke
    Claude Debussy
    Paul Morand
    Djuna Barnes
    Jean Rhys
    A. J. Liebling
    Peter Matthiessen
    Guillaume Apollinaire

Mavis Gallant
Henry Miller
Julian Green
Louis-Ferdinand Céline
Nina Berberova
Ward Just
Marc Chagall
Alastair Gordon
Roland Barthes
George Orwell
Brion Gysin
Jean Rhys
Vladimir Nabokov
William Styron
Julian Green
Jack Kerouac
Léonor Fini
A. J. Liebling
Judi Culbertson & Tom Randall
Nancy Mitford
Ludwig Bemelmans

PARISIANS   31

Jane Kramer
Kate Simon
Marguerite Duras
Richard Bernstein
James Baldwin
Joseph Barry

MEANS OF TRANSPORT   39

Bill Bryson
Edith Wharton
Franz Kafka

Lawrence Osborne
C. W. Gusewelle

PRESENCE OF THE PAST   45

Bill Bryson
Brassaï
John Clellon Holmes
Colette
Waverley Root
James Wright
Brassaï
Julian Green
Judith Moore
Harry Levin
Paul Zweig
Patric Kuh
Robert Hass
Rainer Maria Rilke
Mary McCarthy
Gertrude Stein

SEASONS, RAIN, LIGHT   63

Yvonne de Bremond d'Ars
Raymond Queneau
James Wright
Ned Rorem
Katherine Mansfield
Elizabeth Bishop
Jane Bowles
Edmund White
Cyril Connolly
W. Somerset Maugham
Nina Berberova
Jean Rhys

Albert Camus
Andrew Harvey
Violette Leduc
Galway Kinnell
William Carlos Williams
Jean-Paul Sartre

FOOD   77

Jean Renoir
Romain Gary
Ernest Hemingway
A. J. Liebling
Sylvia Beach
William Faulkner
C. W. Gusewelle
Kate Simon

COLOR   85

Henry Miller
William Wiser

LOVE & SOLACE   89

Andrew Harvey
Guillaume Apollinaire
Frank O'Hara
Nancy Mitford
Max Frisch
Erica Jong
Joseph Barry
Andrew Harvey
John Clellon Holmes
Katherine Anne Porter
Count Alphonse de Toulouse-Lautrec

PARIS HISTORICAL   101

    Herbert Adams Gibbons
    George Seldes
    Josephine Baker & Jo Bouillon
    Janet Flanner
    Al Laney
    Samuel Putnam
    Caresse Crosby
    Jean-Paul Sartre
    Adrienne Monnier
    John Toland
    Jacques-Henri Lartigue
    François Truffaut
    Marcel Ophuls
    E. B. White
    Jacques-Henri Lartigue
    Simone de Beauvoir
    Marguerite Duras
    Gerald Murphy
    Alice Toklas
    Françoise Gilot
    André Malraux
    Mavis Gallant
    Janet Flanner
    Mavis Gallant

A CITY TO DIE IN   123

    Rainer Maria Rilke
    E. V. Lucas
    Louis-Ferdinand Céline
    Ludwig Bemelmans

FIRST PERSON SINGULAR   129

    Alfred Stieglitz
    Harry Crosby

Kay Boyle
Anita Loos
Zelda Fitzgerald
M. F. K. Fisher
Luis Buñuel
Paul Bowles
Henry Miller
André Malraux
André Gide
Jean Cocteau
Paul Bowles
Salvador Dalí
Jessica Mitford
Anonymous
Samuel Steward
Gregory Riley
Truman Capote
Ned Rorem
Janet Flanner
M. F. K. Fisher
Albert Camus
Maya Angelou
Anne Sexton
James Baldwin
Sylvia Plath
Tess Gallagher
Joseph Barry
Carolyn Forché
Violette Leduc
Marc Chagall
Kate Simon

Credits   153
Index of Authors & Places   163

WHEN I WAS FIVE, my father traded in our lives. Our family of four moved from the suburban housing of Southern California to a sixth-floor apartment in Paris' seventh arrondissement. Opting for the Champs de Mars, with its elegant topiary and majestic lawns, in lieu of Disneyland's uninspired flower beds, my parents had brought me, "shy, a traveler," as Czeslaw Milosz wrote of himself, "a young barbarian just come to the capital of the world."

It is not a poetic conceit on my part that in my mind I see the Paris of my childhood in black and white images, singular and evocative. For centuries the City has played out an intricate orchestration—variations on the color gray (all but Payne's gray, as Henry Miller once remarked): wet cobblestone laced with a crepuscular light; slanted, charcoal-colored rooftops; stonework—Louvre, Palais-Royal—darkened by the passage of time; an overcast Parisian sky; and the black and white celluloid images, cultural and political icons of the mid-to-late 1960s.

Now, when I see Paris, its actual burst of color sometimes jars my beloved, carefully imagined City. How to preserve the Paris of my childhood? How to safeguard the City of my imagination, this place in the world called Paris? In the passages I have selected here, I hope to have captured a Paris many readers will recognize, remember, and appreciate.

A Place in the World Called Paris is a collection of over one hundred and seventy fiction and nonfiction excerpts on Paris culled from many of the twentieth century's most distinguished voices: Rainer Maria Rilke, William Styron, Colette, M. F. K. Fisher, John Berger, Czeslaw Milosz, Thomas Mann, Paul Auster, Mavis Gallant, Nancy Mitford, Elizabeth Bishop, and Mary McCarthy, among many others. Paris—this "most capital capital," as Janet Flanner once called it—is a city of infinite variety: exalted, fanciful, as well as somber with the very misery of existence. These literary passages reflect this "variety" and suggest a synthesis of Parisian history, ephemera, sensory experience, and personal memoir. Drawings by artist Miles Hyman are also included to reflect distinct Parisian archetypes: a stone urn from the Tuileries Gardens; a bistro setting; a view of the Orsay Museum clock; the detail of a doorway—images that are as immediately recognizable as the authors whose text they complement.

STEVEN BARCLAY

FOREWORD

MASHA DREAMS OF GOING to live in Paris. An angelic writer of plays and
short stories wrote a play about her and her two sisters, how they longed to
break free of their stifling provincial destinies, and since the writer, Russian,
made Masha and kin Russian too, it seemed more plausible to have them dream
of going to live one day in Moscow. But, actually, it was Paris.

To hell with the provinces. That's where people have expectations
about how you are supposed to be. Capital cities are where your neighbors aren't
necessarily neighbors, where hardly anybody cares about what you do, and where
you have a crack at becoming, according to your modest or immodest hopes,
what you really want to be. Maybe all you want is not to do anything for a while:
just struggle with the language (no encouragement from the locals there!), have
sensual adventures, gape at the buildings, browse in the bookstores, hang out,
enjoy being ignored. Provinciality being a universal condition, every capital city
is also a capital of provincialism. What foreigners relished about Paris was that
it was so drenched in itself.

A lover of cities is usually polygamous. So let's admit that Paris is hardly
the only European city with stunningly seductive architecture, food, babble, and
traditions of leisure. And, as for ancient credentials, it can't compare with, say,
Rome. But no city has offered such a spectrum of imagined and, sometimes, real
fulfillments. Exile's Paris, drinker's Paris, artist's Paris, student's Paris, champion
moviegoer's Paris, sexual quester's Paris . . . the Paris offered to the imagination
of foreigners was like water, filling every form.

In the play, it seems clear that Masha and Olga and Irina will never get to Moscow. As it happens, the real Masha did get to Paris: for a month when she was eighteen, then for almost a year when she was twenty-four. If Paris had long ceased to be what first fired her adolescent imagination—Paris of *Les Enfants du Paradis*, the nineteenth-century village of lovers' heartbreak and theatrical street life—it was still Paris enough to provide experience of the most pleasurable outsiderliness. A routine in Paris, that was heaven. Awake in your *chambre de bonne* at eleven, lunch in a cheap bistro, afternoon at the Old Navy or some other not so modish café on the Boulevard St-Germain, a baguette sandwich before adjourning to the first (or the second, or the third) film at the Cinémathèque, off with your chums to a bar with jazz or a bar that was simply, properly, *louche*; then, not before three in the morning and, if you were doing your job right, not alone, to bed.

Once upon a time, to be in Paris—if you were a foreigner; certainly if you were an American—was itself a kind of victory. But it seemed presumptuous, if you weren't French, to go on living in Paris. Moscow, for instance, was awful, but it was, well, real. And, after all, the playwright's Masha was Russian. So the real Masha, having prolonged her Paris fix as long as possible, settled for her own capital. But she returned to Paris, gratefully, again and again.

SUSAN SONTAG

CONDITIONS OF ITS GREATNESS

Bypassing rue Descartes

I descended toward the Seine, shy, a traveler,
A young barbarian just come to the capital of the world.

Bypassing Rue Descartes
Czeslaw Milosz
1980

Of an August day in Paris the choice hour is from six to seven in the evening. The choice promenade is the Seine between the Pont Alexandre III and the Pont de l'Archevêché. If one walks down the quays of the Rive Gauche toward Notre-Dame first, and then turns back on the Rive Droite, he has the full glory of the setting sun before him and reaches the Place de la Concorde just in time to get a glimpse up the Champs Élysées toward the Arc de Triomphe as the last light of day is disappearing. I am not yet old enough to have taken this walk a thousand times, but when I have I am sure that it will present the same fascination, the same stirring of soul, the same exaltation that it does to-day.

Choose, if you will, your August sunset at the seashore or in the mountains. There you have nature *unspoiled,* you say. But is there not a revelation of God through animate as well as inanimate creation? If we can have the sun going down on both at the same time, why not? Notre-Dame may be surpassed by other churches, even in France. But Notre-Dame, in its setting on the island that is the heart and center of this city, historically and architecturally that high water mark of human endeavor, cannot be surpassed. Standing on the bridge between the Morgue and the Ile St-Louis, and looking towards the setting sun, one sees the most perfect blending of the creation of God and the creation of the creatures of God that the world affords. And it is not because I have not seen the sunset from the Acropolis, from the Janiculum, from the Golden Horn, and from the steps of El Akbar, that I make this statement. Athens, Rome, Constantinople, Cairo—these have been, but Paris is.

Paris Reborn
HERBERT ADAMS GIBBONS
1915

EVERY CITY HAS A SEX and an age which have nothing to do with demography . . . Paris, I believe, is a man in his 20's in love with an older woman. Somewhat spoilt by his mother, not so much with kisses as with purchases.

Keeping a Rendezvous
JOHN BERGER
1991

I HAD NEVER LOOKED at a street as Henry does: every doorway, every lamp, every window, every courtyard, every shop, every object in the shop, every café, every hidden-away bookshop, hidden-away antique shop, every news vendor, every lottery-ticket vendor, every blind man, every beggar, every clock, every church, every whore house, every wineshop, every shop where they sell erotica and transparent underwear, the circus, the night-club singer, the strip tease, the girlie shows, the penny movies in the arcade, the bal musettes, the artists' ball, the apache quarters, the flea market, the gypsy cart, the markets in the early morning.

Diary of Anaïs Nin
ANAÏS NIN
1932

LIVING QUIETLY AS I DO, I never realize how many affectionate friends I do have in the world, and the manifestations of that friendship on such occasions bewilder me even more than they gladden me. It was even wilder in Paris. The reception at the Ritz, organized by the publisher of *Docteur Faustus,* was a tumult; for three hours I had to sign books in a *librairie* while people stood *in line* on the street under police supervision; and the lecture in the Sorbonne had to be transferred to the large *amphithéâtre.* Two thousand people came—it is a long time since anything like that occurred, I was told—and the conduct of this crowd too was extraordinary. I find it foolish, for fame is founded on foolish and confused reasons; but I report it because it may amuse you.

What it leaves me with is fatigue and a sense of *humbug,* but at the same time a quiet feeling of joy that in some way I can be something to people. Incidentally, it had literally slipped my mind how beautiful Paris is. A glorious city! It happened to be the day of the Maid, with a grand parade in front of her monument outside our hotel, and at night the architectural complex from Notre-Dame to Sacré-Coeur was enchantingly illuminated with spotlights. Magnificent.

From a letter sent to Agnes E. Meyer
THOMAS MANN
1950

WHAT IS UNIQUE in Baudelaire's poetry is that the images of women and death are permeated by a third, that of Paris. The Paris of his poems is a submerged city, more submarine than subterranean. The chthonic elements of the city—its topographical formation, the old deserted bed of the Seine— doubtless left their impression on his work. Yet what is decisive in Baudelaire's "deathly idyll" of the city is a social, modern substratum. Modernity is a main accent in his poetry. He shatters the ideal as spleen *(Spleen et Idéal)*. But it is precisely modernity that is always quoting primeval history. This happens here through the ambiguity attending the social relationships and products of this epoch. Ambiguity is the pictorial image of dialectics, the law of dialectics seen at a standstill. This standstill is utopia and dialectic image therefore a dream image. Such an image is presented by the pure commodity: as fetish. Such an image are the arcades, which are both house and stars. Such an image is the prostitute, who is saleswoman and wares in one.

Reflections
WALTER BENJAMIN
1955

THERE IS ANOTHER QUALITY, inseparably connected with Paris, which may be termed "vitality"—merely an expression for those who do not know Paris, but for those who have spent only a few days there, the finest experience which the city offers, a something which pervades the people, the surroundings, and the whole atmosphere. Moreover, the Paris of today keeps alive its past history, and this rare unity produces a great wealth of variety, adding profundity to largeness and fulness.

Paris and Environs
GRIEBEN'S GUIDE BOOK
1929

MY PROBLEM WAS SIMPLE: I had a hangover and I needed time with my own wounds before coping with anyone else's, and so, leaving Shirley still asleep, I went out and walked, looking at the cheap little hotels, and imagining absolutely eventless days of morning-coffee, croissant, and the Trib, wandering remote arrondissements through pastis-tinted afternoons, chanson-bars where gypsy-fingers spidered along the frets of huge guitars, and early nights of neon-flicker on the ceiling, and none of those long thoughts about death and change that gave so many Americans in those days a vaguely haunted look. There are backstreets in Paris that offer the careless oblivion some of us long for when life has turned a cold corner, for Paris still receives the miserable stranger like a good-hearted prostitute of all the myths: you can always sleep on her floor.

A Wake in the Streets of Paris
JOHN CLELLON HOLMES
1987

I'M GLAD TO HEAR that you like Paris; the right way of course is to take it as a place and a tradition, rather than as a congeries of people, who are mostly futile and timewasting, except when you want to pass an evening agreeably in a café. The chief danger about Paris is that it is such a strong stimulus, and like most stimulants incites to rushing about and produces a pleasant illusion of great mental activity rather than the solid results of hard work. When I was living there years ago I had only the genuine stimulus of the place, and not the artificial stimulus of the people, as I knew no one whatever, in the literary and artistic world, as a companion—knew them rather as spectacles, listened to, at rare occasions, but never spoken to.

From a letter sent to Robert McAlmon
T. S. ELIOT
1921

Things felt oddly bigger to me in Paris. The sky was more present than in New York, its whims more fragile. I found myself drawn to it, and for the first day or two I watched it constantly—sitting in my hotel room and studying the clouds, waiting for something to happen. These were northern clouds, the dream clouds that are always changing, massing up into huge gray mountains, discharging brief showers, dissipating, gathering again, rolling across the sun, refracting the light in ways that always seem different. The Paris sky has its own laws, and they function independently of the city below. If the buildings appear solid, anchored in the earth, indestructible, the sky is vast and amorphous, subject to constant turmoil. For the first week, I felt as though I had been turned upside-down. This was an old world city, and it had nothing to do with New York—with its slow skies and chaotic streets, its bland clouds and aggressive buildings. I had been displaced, and it made me suddenly unsure of myself. I felt my grip loosening, and at least once an hour I had to remind myself why I was there.

> *The Locked Room*
> PAUL AUSTER
> 1986

We rolled into the station Saint-Lazare about four o'clock in the afternoon and drove immediately to the Hôtel Continental. My benefactor, humouring my curiosity and enthusiasm, which seemed to please him very much, suggested that we take a short walk before dinner. We stepped out of the hotel and turned to the right into the rue de Rivoli. When the vista of the Place de la Concorde and the Champs-Élysées suddenly burst upon me, I could hardly credit my own eyes. I shall attempt no such supererogatory task as a description of Paris. I wish only to give briefly the impressions which that wonderful city made upon me. It impressed me as the perfect and perfectly beautiful city; and even after I had been there for some time, and seen not only its avenues and palaces, but its most squalid alleys and hovels, this impression was not weakened. Paris became for me a charmed spot, and whenever I have returned there, I have fallen under the spell, a spell which compels admiration for all of its manners and customs and justification of even its follies and sins.

Autobiography of an Ex-Coloured Man
JAMES WELDON JOHNSON
1927

I NEEDED PARIS. It was a feast, a grand carnival of imagery, and immediately everything good there seemed to offer sublimation to those inner desires that had for so long been hampered by racism back in America. For the first time in my life I was relaxing from tension and pressure. My thoughts, continually rampaging against racial conditions, were suddenly becoming as peaceful as snowflakes. Slowly a curtain was dropping between me and those soiled years.

Voices in the Mirror
GORDON PARKS
1990

P L A C E

Of all the Seine bridges the Pont des Arts is the pleasantest to sit or walk on; it is reserved for pedestrians and is really a promenade pitched between sky and water for students, nursemaids, children, old gentlemen, and for painters having another go at the classical view of the Pont-Neuf and the Ile de la Cité, picking out the light on the Tour St-Jacques, struggling to get that flaking-gray shade of the river buildings. Nothing sacred or secular, joyous or macabre escapes the inflection of French irony. I was chatting with a plump and rosy young man who is in charge of the small lifesaving station that is cozily shaded by the trees close to the bridge. Every couple of days, he said, people jump off the Pont des Arts or the quays close by the river. It is the bridge, he said, most esteemed by those wishing to make a show of ending their lives. "But never at night," he added. "No Frenchman ever commits suicide at night. He wants to be seen doing it. *Il veut se faire un drame.*" The stagelike elevation of the bridge, he said, with its fine view of the Louvre on one side and the dome of the Institut on the other, contributing their suggestions of art and poetry, makes the spot appropriate. But between his little boat moored below and the skiffs of the river fire station on the other side of the bridge, he said that the chances of a fatal success were small. The morgue, by the way, so conscientiously visited by the French Naturalist school and the painters of the nineteenth century, has been moved from the Ile de la Cité. A garden is there now.

Down the Seine
V. S. Pritchett
1963

In haste: for outside is the Luxembourg, shimmering: so how can I hold out any longer at my desk?

From a letter written to Countess M.
Rainer Maria Rilke
1920

Mon cher Inghel,

I beg to acknowledge receipt of your letter of the 25th instant—as my wine-merchant would say. I enjoyed reading it enormously because of your exact, ironic description of the Luxembourg gardens . . . I love them, all the same. They represent a fine period of French history and if those who walk around in them are rather a special breed, they're preferable, by and large, to the smart "cocktail" habitués of the Bois de Boulogne. After all, the poor Luxembourg isn't responsible for the terrible statues with which our artistic leaders have thought fit to decorate it. But what a delightful walk it is along the "allée des Reines"!

From a letter sent to D. E. Inghelbrecht
Claude Debussy
1915

Of all the Paris gardens those of the Luxembourg have the fullest complement of dreamers. It is not only the children who build their Spanish castles among its paths, but the aimless intellectuals of Bohemia, too, for whom there are no winter sports, no country holidays, no trips to the seaside. Giraudoux and I used to wander there when we were students. Balzac, in his *Grand Homme de Province à Paris* speaks of the "poor children from the country whose sole recreation is to wander the long paths of the Luxembourg, and look at the pretty women with sidelong glances and beating hearts." One meets many a loiterer muttering his rhymes (they still believe in rhymes!) or pondering some new idea (they still believe in ideas!). On tilted chairs beneath the chestnuts young women read their Bergson. Students, men and women, hurry across the Gardens on their way from the Sorbonne, all afire for life. But in the autumn their pace is slower: among the few dead leaves that the gardeners have left them, they saunter with a sense of pleasure that they do not trouble to analyze, pleasure that is the gift of romantic reverie.

Full of instruction, too, the Gardens are for youth. Before the statues of the Queens of France you can see many a mother hearing her young scholar's history lesson, and bright mornings are curiously mixed in memory with George Sand seated on the grass, the Comtesse de Ségur perched up on her pole, and Verlaine emerging from the vase that forms his pedestal.

Nature here is intellectualized, a thing of neat arrangement, of flights of steps, of architecture and clipped trees. The Palace of the Senate is not sufficient to keep the wind from the fountains, and here and there one comes on a little girl crying for her tiny boat marooned. But she can always be comforted by the pears carefully wrapped in neat paper bags as though dressed in their best Sunday clothes.

Paris to the Life
PAUL MORAND
1933

FELIX, CARRYING TWO VOLUMES on the life of the Bourbons, called the next day at the *Hôtel Récamier.* Miss Vote was not in. Four afternoons in succession he called, only to be told that she had just left. On the fifth, turning the corner of the *rue Bonaparte,* he ran into her.

Removed from her setting—the plants that had surrounded her, the melancholy red velvet of the chairs and the curtains, the sound, weak and nocturnal, of the birds—she yet carried the quality of the "way back" as animals do. She suggested that they should walk together in the gardens of the Luxembourg toward which her steps had been directed when he addressed her. They walked in the bare chilly gardens and Felix was happy. He felt that he could talk to her, tell her anything, though she herself was so silent.

Nightwood
DJUNA BARNES
1937

MONTPARNASSE WAS FULL OF THESE STREETS and they were often inordinately long. You could walk for hours. The Rue Vaugirard, for instance. Marya had never yet managed to reach the end of the Rue Vaugirard, which was a very respectable thoroughfare on the whole. But if you went far enough towards Grenelle and then turned down side streets . . .

Quartet
JEAN RHYS
1928

THE RESTAURANT DES BEAUX-ARTS, where I did my early research, was across the street from the École des Beaux-Arts, and not, in fact, precisely in my quarter, which was that of the university proper, a good half mile away, on the other side of the Boulevard Saint-Germain. It was a half mile which made as much difference as the border between France and Switzerland. The language was the same, but not the inhabitants. Along the Rue Bonaparte there were antiquarians, and in the street leading off it were practitioners of the ancillary arts—picture framers and bookbinders. The bookshops of the Rue Bonaparte, of which there were many, dealt in fine editions and rare books, instead of the used textbooks and works of erudition that predominated around the university. The students of the Beaux-Arts were only a small element of the population of the neighborhood, and they were a different breed from the students of the Boulevard Saint-Michel and its tributaries, such as the Rue de l'École de Médecine, where I lived. They were older and seemingly in easier circumstances. I suspected them of commercial art and of helping Italians to forge antiques. Because there was more money about, and because the quarter had a larger proportion of adult, experienced eaters, it was better territory for restaurants than the immediate neighborhood of the Sorbonne.

Between Meals
A. J. LIEBLING
1959

Sand rose early the next morning and went out to get his breakfast. He went inland from the quai, up the rue Saint-André-des-Arts, and turned off into the rue de Buci. There, from his table in a small café, he would observe the Buci market place and the faces of his new neighborhood. These were very different from the Right Bank faces, less obsequious and much less disagreeable, and there were representatives of every class on this noisy common ground. He had a comfortable feeling of being one of them, and, after his coffee, strolled up and down among the stalls. From there he wandered down the rue de Seine and came out on the river opposite the Louvre.

Turning, he surveyed by daylight the maze into which Rudi had led him the evening before, but there was no sign of it. On his left loomed the massive Institut and down to his right the open garden of the Beaux Arts. He was once again in the public Paris, the impersonal Paris, and his new quarter, personal and unpredictable, lurked somewhere behind these facades. He moved up the quai and re-entered the quarter, with excitement and misgiving, by the river end of the rue des Grands-Augustins.

Partisans
PETER MATTHIESSEN
1955

I SAW THIS MORNING a pretty street whose name I've forgotten
Fresh and clean it was the bugle of the sunlight The directors
the workers and the lovely shorthand typists Pass through it
four times a day from Monday morning to Saturday evening In
the morning the siren wails there three times A querulous bell
yelps there towards midday The lettering on the signs and walls
The nameplates the notices shriek like parrots I love the grace
of this industrial street Located in Paris between the Rue
Aumont-Thiéville and the Avenue des Ternes

Zone
GUILLAUME APOLLINAIRE
1913

SANDOR SPECK'S FIRST ART GALLERY in Paris was on the Right Bank, near the church of Ste-Elisabeth, on a street too narrow for cars. When his block was wiped off the map to make way for a five-story garage, Speck crossed the Seine to the shadow of Saint-Julien-le-Pauvre, where he set up shop in a picturesque slum protected by law from demolition. When this gallery was blown up by Basque separatists, who had mistaken it for a travel

agency exploiting the beauty of their coast, he collected his insurance money
and moved to the Faubourg Saint-Germain.

Speck's Idea
MAVIS GALLANT
1979

I COME UPON THE SQUARE DU FURSTEMBERG. Have I ever
spoken of it before? Here is where I should like to take rooms. A deserted spot,
bleak, spectral at night, containing in the center four black trees which have not
yet begun to blossom. These four bare trees have the poetry of T. S. Eliot. They
are intellectual trees, nourished by the stones, swaying with a rhythm cerebral,
the lines punctuated by dots and dashes, by asterisks and exclamation points.

Letters to Emil
HENRY MILLER
1930

DELACROIX'S STUDIO in the tiny Furstemberg Square. The
delightful sunken garden that is so good to sit in, shaded by trees, in the silence
cut by the breeze on this fine summer's day, only yards from the deafening
boulevard Saint-Germain. All around us, old houses with open windows, and
those windows quite black. Watercolours by Delacroix, Huet, Riesener, Hugo,
dreams in every direction. This oasis in our century that is so wretchedly devoid
of poetry. A pale-blue sky above our heads, with clouds floating in it like puffs
of steam.

Paris
JULIAN GREEN
1992

W<small>E LEFT THE RUE DE</small> B<small>ABYLONE</small> to open another shop, to try our luck again. This time it was the Passage des Beresinas, between the Stock Exchange and the Boulevards. Our living quarters were over the shop, three rooms connected by a spiral staircase. My mother was always limping up and down those stairs. Tip-tap-plunk, tip-tap-plunk. She'd hold on to the banister.

Death on the Installment Plan
L<small>OUIS</small>-F<small>ERDINAND</small> C<small>ÉLINE</small>
1952

I <small>STAND FOR A LONG TIME</small> on the Place de la Concorde, where there is as much sky as in a Russian rye field or a corn field in Kansas.

The Italics Are Mine
N<small>INA</small> B<small>ERBEROVA</small>
1992

T<small>HEY WALKED ACROSS</small> the bridge to the Place de la Concorde, standing a moment to admire its proportions and the magic sweep up the Champs-Élysées to the Arc de Triomphe. Then they struck off down rue de Rivoli to rue de Castiglione, leading to Place Vendôme. Carroll stopped several times, peering up the straight line of rue de Rivoli to its vanishing point. The apartments facing the Tuileries put him in mind of a mountain face made of stone and glass. It was perfection, so composed and harmonious that it was like something found in nature.

The Translator
W<small>ARD</small> J<small>UST</small>
1992

ONLY THE GREAT DISTANCE that separates Paris from my native town prevented me from going back home immediately or at least after a week, or a month.

I even wanted to invent a holiday of some kind, just as an excuse to go home.

It was the Louvre that put an end to all this wavering. When I walked round the Veronese room and the rooms where the Manets, Delacroix, and Courbets are, I wanted nothing more.

My Life
MARC CHAGALL
1931

IN PARIS A BUILDING is never just a building. New public architecture gets served up as a gourmand's feast of allegory and national politics. I. M. Pei's pyramid at the Louvre is not just a new entrance to an old museum but a central eye for all of Paris, regenerating all that is old, redefining the entire city around its single glass point like a magic crystal in Superman's Fortress of Solitude.

Architecture View
ALASTAIR GORDON
1991

MAUPASSANT OFTEN LUNCHED at the restaurant in the tower, though he didn't care much for the food: *It's the only place in Paris,* he used to say, *where I don't have to see it.* And it's true that you must take endless precautions, in Paris, not to see the Eiffel Tower; whatever the season, through mist and cloud, on overcast days or in sunshine, in rain—wherever you are, whatever the landscape of roofs, domes, or branches separating you from it, *the Tower is there;*

incorporated into daily life until you can no longer grant it any specific attribute, determined merely to persist, like a rock or the river, it is as literal as a phenomenon of nature whose meaning can be questioned to infinity but whose existence is incontestable. There is virtually no Parisian glance it fails to *touch* at some time of day; at the moment I begin writing these lines about it, the Tower is there, in front of me, framed by my window; and at the very moment the January night blurs it, apparently trying to make it invisible, to deny its presence, two little lights come on, winking gently as they revolve at its very tip: all this night, too, it will be there, connecting me above Paris to each of my friends that I know are seeing it: with it we all comprise a shifting figure of which it is the steady center: the Tower is friendly.

The Eiffel Tower
ROLAND BARTHES
1979

LIFE IN THE QUARTER. Our *bistro*, for instance, at the foot of the Hôtel des Trois Moineaux. A tiny brick-floored room, half underground, with wine-sodden tables, and a photograph of a funeral inscribed "*Crédit est mort*"; and red-sashed workmen carving sausage with big jack-knives; and Madame F., a splendid Auvergnat peasant woman with the face of a strong-minded cow, drinking Malaga all day "for her stomach"; and games of dice for *apéritifs;* and songs about "*Les Fraises et Les Framboises*," and about Madelon, who said, "*Comment épouser un soldat, moi qui aime tout le régiment?*"; and extraordinarily public love-making.

Down and Out in Paris and London
GEORGE ORWELL
1933

Madame Rachou who ran our fleabitten rooming-house with "inflexible authority," as William Burroughs said, was "the perfect landlady" and our guardian angel. She had no use for the police, none at all. If she was "tender" with us, she was "pugnacious" with them, determined not to let them set foot in the place, not even her little bistro on the street with its already old fashioned zinc-topped bar. She may have had to splash out a free drink or two of her sour white wine for a plain clothes cop now and then but if she did, we never knew it. She was so small she had to stand on an overturned winecase, the better to keep an eye on things. She could peer out into our narrow little street through her aspidistra plants and lace curtains to see who was coming or going.

The Beat Hotel, Paris
Brion Gysin
1977

Halfway up the Boulevard Montparnasse is a little café called the Zanzi-Bar. It is not one of those popular places swarming with the shingled and long-legged and their partners, who all wear picturesque collars and an incredibly contemptuous expression. No, it is small, half-empty, cheapish. Coffee costs five centimes less than in the Rotonde, for instance. It is a place to know of. It is not gay, except on the rare occasions when some festive soul asks the patron for the Valencia record and puts a ten centimes piece into the gramophone slot.

Here, one evening at eleven o'clock, sat a Lady drinking her fourth *fine à l'eau* and thinking how much she disliked human beings in general and those who pitied her in particular. For it was her deplorable habit, when she felt very blue indeed, to proceed slowly up the right-hand side of the Boulevard, taking a *fine à l'eau*—that is to say a brandy and soda—at every second café she passed. There are so many cafés that the desired effect could be obtained without walking very far, and by thus moving from one to the other she managed to avoid both the curious stares of the waiters and the disadvantage of not accurately knowing just how drunk she was.

In the Rue de L'Arrivée
JEAN RHYS
1927

My STAY AT THE STEPANOVS' had been supposed to last a couple of weeks; it lasted two months. At first I felt comparatively well, or at least comfortable and refreshed, but a new sleeping pill which had worked so well at its beguiling stage began refusing to cope with certain reveries which, as suggested subsequently by an incredible sequel, I should have succumbed to like a man and got done with no matter how; instead of that I took advantage of Dolly's removal to England to find a new dwelling for my miserable carcass. This was a bed-sitting-room in a shabby but quiet tenement house on the Left Bank, "at the corner of rue St. Supplice," says my pocket diary with grim imprecision. An ancient cupboard of sorts contained a primitive shower bath; but there were no other facilities. Going out two or three times a day for a meal, or a cup of coffee, or an extravagant purchase at a delicatessen, afforded me a small *distraction*. In the next block I found a cinema that specialized in old horse operas and a tiny brothel with four whores ranging in age from eighteen to thirty-eight, the youngest being also the plainest.

I was to spend many years in Paris, tied to that dismal city by threads of a Russian writer's livelihood. Nothing then, and nothing now, in backcast, has or had for me any of the spell that enthralled my compatriots. I am not thinking of the blood spot on the darkest stone of its darkest street; that is *hors-concours* in the way of horror; I just mean that I regarded Paris, with its gray-toned days and charcoal nights, merely as the chance setting for the most authentic and faithful joys of my life: the colored phrase in my mind under the drizzle, the white page under the desk lamp awaiting me in my humble home.

Look at the Harlequins!
VLADIMIR NABOKOV
1974

In PARIS ON A CHILLY EVENING late in October of 1985 I first became fully aware that the struggle with the disorder in my mind—a struggle which had engaged me for several months—might have a fatal outcome. The moment of revelation came as the car in which I was riding moved down the rain-slick street not far from the Champs-Élysées and slid past a dully glowing neon sign that read HÔTEL WASHINGTON. I had not seen that hotel in nearly thirty-five years, since the spring of 1952, when for several nights it had become my initial Parisian roosting place. In the first few months of my *Wanderjahr*, I had come down to Paris from Copenhagen, and landed at the Hôtel Washington through the whimsical determination of a New York travel agent. In those days the hotel was one of the many damp, plain hosteleries made for tourists, chiefly American, of very modest means who, if they were like me—colliding nervously for the first time with the French and their droll kinks—would always remember how the exotic bidet, positioned solidly in the drab bedroom, along with the toilet far down the ill-lit hallway, virtually defined the chasm between Gallic and Anglo-Saxon cultures.

Darkness Visible
WILLIAM STYRON
1989

THE TUILERIES GARDENS disgraced by wooden horses, kiddies' trains, and a large Bavarian casino in which a group of rustics in leather trousers are yodelling to four customers. Somewhere else, Mozart melodies bellow deafeningly from a radio.

I walk on as far as the Opera House, where I had intended to pay a quick visit to the Café de la Paix. However, it is closed for alterations. I tremble at what that implies. . . . On the boulevard a typical holiday crowd, obviously with time on its hands, hanging about, queuing outside the cinemas, wretched and depressing. I hate the boulevard, where I sense the presence of an almost supernatural boredom.

And what shall I say of the entrails that the Beaubourg Palace exhibits with the idiotic satisfaction of a toddler baring its stomach? You do, from the third floor, have a marvellous view of Paris, but first you must pass through the middle of those monstrous sky-blue tubes and all the rest of the pipework bedizening the exterior.

Paris
JULIAN GREEN
1992

FIRST THINGS FIRST.

The altar in La Madelaine is a gigantic marble sculpt of her (Mary Magdalena) as big as a city block and surrounded by angels and archangels. She holds out her hand in a gesture Michelangeloesque. The angels have huge wings dripping. The place is a whole city block long. It's a long narrow building of a church, one of the strangest. No spires, no Gothic, but I suppose Greek temple style. (Why on earth would you, or did you, expect me to go see the Eiffel Tower made of Bucky Buckmaster's steel ribs and ozone? How dull can you get riding an elevator and getting the mumps from being a quarter mile high in the air? I already done that orf the Hempire State Building at night in the mist with my editor.)

Satori in Paris
JACK KEROUAC
1966

I HAVE LONGTIME IMAGINED, since childhood, that banks were "very adult" places, severe, orderly, where one always had to wait standing up. Very young, I'd never have dreamed that one day I might choose of my own free will, to have anything to do with one of these aloof buildings. The money which I began to earn in life had a way, at first, of casually finding its way in between the pages of favorite books, in boxes just emptied of chocolates or candied chestnuts, into a dress shoe (which was too narrow and pinched a little) and even behind the stretcher bars of my paintings (I'd just begun painting with oils). At times I forgot where I had put it, this money of mine. . . . But when my income increased I began raking up and stuffing the bills into a rose-colored scarf which was called *il topo rosso* (it was a traveling companion, of course). By turns it grew fat or thin, this little rose-colored mouse. To see that it was fed all I had to do was accept a portrait commission, do a wallpaper or material design, create the graphics for a deck of playing cards. . . .

One autumn day, the friend who accompanied me on the morning stroll remembered that he had to "stop by his bank" and asked me to wait for him a moment near the black torch-bearer statues behind the Opéra. My conversation with these beautiful creatures started to lag; the wait began to get on my nerves so I dared enter the great formal portals of this Société Générale bank (the very name intrigued me: what "society"? what "general"?).

My friend was no where in sight. How to find him in this extraordinary place where an enormous circular counter lured a crowd of people (some inside, others outside its sprawling circumference). My attention was quickly magnetized, overhead, by the immense cabochon of the stained-glass cupola which seemed like a Lalique jewel, through which autumnal opalescences were shining under a pale sun, illuminating the inner ridge of the rotunda with its decorative figures of beautiful, solemn women personifying the cities of France.

A little worried not seeing my friend anywhere about, I began to describe him to an impassive stranger in uniform, who soberly answered: "In the safe!"

And I descended the sinuous winding staircase until I reached a rotunda of zebra-striped mosaic just as the enormous round portal of shiny copper and steel silently opened to reveal my friend.

Seeing me so curious, so captivated, he smilingly suggested that he go back with me through the glowing, armored ring (exactly as I had always imagined entering the shell of the Nautilus which protects the sealed-in kingdom of Captain Nemo).

I found myself in a five story, blue-grey underground, a metropolis washed by streaming light rays, where one could barely make out the shadowy figures bent over double desks with opal-moonstone panels and brass appearing to be of solid gold (Gallé? Bugatti?).

It was this palace of marvels, with a magic life of its own, yet at the same time totally functional (the perfect definition of that historical transition called *Fin de Siècle*). That became . . . I willed it thus . . ."my bank."

Société Générale
LÉONOR FINI
1986

ONCE THAT SUMMER they took me, unforgettably, to Napoléon's tomb, where the gold light, the marble, and the massed battle flags made an image of Napoléonic glory that has always helped me understand the side of Stendhal that is least rational. If brief exposures to the glories of the Empire, a hundred years later, could so dazzle me, I find it easy to pardon the effect upon a lieutenant of dragoons eighteen years old, riding in the midst of the Sixth Light Dragoons, uniform bottle-green, red waist-coat, white breeches, helmet with crest, horsetail, and red cockade.

Between Meals
A. J. LIEBLING
1959

PARIS IS FAMOUS FOR HER CROISSANTS, her art treasures, and her general cachet, but perhaps she is less well known for her necrography. Yet nothing illustrates the slender line between life and death so well as the cemeteries of Paris. Stone figures seem to start up from their beds as if hearing a noise, or dance as if they had been turned to marble without warning. To visit these burial grounds is to be struck with wonder.

Permanent Parisians
JUDI CULBERTSON & TOM RANDALL
1986

THE SERVANT SAID that M. le Duc had just gone out with Madame la Duchesse, but that he would be back in about an hour. Linda said she would wait, and he showed her into Fabrice's sitting-room. She took off her hat, and wandered restlessly about. She had been here several times before, with Fabrice, and it had seemed, after her brilliantly sunny flat, a little dismal. Now that she was alone in it she began to be aware of the extreme beauty of the room, a grave and solemn beauty which penetrated her. It was very high, rectangular in shape, with grey boiseries and cherry-coloured brocade curtains. It looked into a courtyard and never could get a ray of sunshine, that was not the plan. This was a civilized interior, it had nothing to do with out of doors. Every object in it was perfect. The furniture had the severe lines and excellent proportions of 1780, there was a portrait by Lancret of a lady with a parrot on her wrist, a bust of the same lady by Bouchardon, a carpet like the one in Linda's flat, but larger and grander, with a huge coat of arms in the middle. A high carved bookcase contained nothing but French classics bound in contemporary morocco, with the Sauveterre crest, and, open on a map table, lay a copy of Redoute's roses.

The Pursuit of Love
NANCY MITFORD
1949

In an old house in Paris
That was covered with vines
Lived twelve little girls
In two straight lines.
They left the house at half-past nine
In two straight lines, in rain or shine.
The smallest one was MADELINE.

Madeline's Christmas
LUDWIG BEMELMANS
1956

PARISIANS

THE CANONS OF GOOD TASTE were writ in a couple of arrondissements in Paris and circulated through France, like copies of the Code Napoléon to provincial courtrooms. Every Frenchman knew exactly what good taste was—and who had it and on what authority—and tried to emulate it. There was really no such thing as different tastes for different Frenchmen. There was only Taste in its variably successful—or unsuccessful—refractions. The French might mark their status with displays of taste, sprinkling their lives with "taste" the way a dog marks territory, but the field in France did not leave much room for eccentricity or invention. It was not a question of whether Henri II or early Memphis but of whether the piece was family furniture or bought on the sly from a distant brocanteur and passed off as the real article. In a way, the French have taste the way other people have gods or despots. The fact of an authorized, official good taste reassures them. They would be anxious without it, because their articles of taste are like articles of faith—not meant for improvisation but firm and aggressive, like good haircuts or well-cut suits or the right flowers on the table. They are a kind of controlling principle in most Frenchmen's lives, emblems of Frenchness that unite and identify a people. A hundred years ago those people invented the designer. Now they have invented the designer's initial. It is a way of saying "La France, c'est Coco Chanel"—or Yves Saint-Laurent or Louis Vuitton—"et Coco Chanel, c'est moi."

Prisoners of Taste
JANE KRAMER
1989

FOR HOTEL RESTING you might try the radio. Most stations, French or foreign, will give you the universal adolescent bleating you will find at home. "France Culture" is something quite else, a set of verbal mosaics that make an idealized self-portrait, not necessarily what you think you see, but what the intellectual Parisian thinks he sees: the 19th century stormy-haired thinker and poet; vibrant, searching, golden-tongued, with a restless, devouring interest in things of the mind and, at the same time, devoted to love, mostly as self-immolation.

In the early morning, when the air is not heavy with carefully enunciated Latin lessons, you might hear a lecture in stately detail on the difference between a puma and a jaguar, or a physics lecture surrounded by splinters of electronic music, or reading from the works of a 15th century chronicler and poet. It might be a report on recent American literature with evaluations of Saul Belleau and Jean Cheevaire, an old travel piece on Mozambique with folklorique music thrumming and ululating behind it or a description of the circumcision rites of remote African tribes described by a dry, rustling voice like the crumbling of yellowed paper. Or, you might hear a discussion of cigarette smoking and lung cancer, tactfully timed—8 A.M.—for an hour when few people can face life, much less death.

One of the favorites of the later morning hours is the long interview with the half-forgotten, elderly poet. For its length and detail it is peculiarly uninformative, probably because the questions are peculiar. The elderly gentleman's mind and creative sensibilities are explored by means of "What military figure do you most admire? Who is your favorite hero? Heroine? Writer? Painter? What are your favorite colors? Your favorite music? If you weren't a poet what would you like to have been?" And the patient old man makes polite, wordy answers to the high school yearbook questions.

The afternoon can bring a reading of Hemingway's *Old Man and the Sea* whose sparse syllables as translated into French and spoken by a member of the

Comédie-Française become gilded, rounded Baroque. The flesh may be that of Papa, but the voice is that of Racine.

In the late afternoon (particularly effective in the slow, sweet, sad summer twilights) comes love, rueful, lorn, tenderly clutching amorous thorns to its bosom. The tunes are often long tuneless recitatives of a hoarse, soft breathing in a minor key, the voice that oddly androgynous French voice which might be a man's high tenor or a woman's low mezzo, and always a bit rough as if passion were ripping the singer's throat.

If all this doesn't interest you and you become impatient with opera and symphonic programs that carry little music and too much program note, a melange of information, opinion and sentimental biography ("A's life was saddened by an unrequited love which is reflected in his use of minor thirds"), you might choose to improve your French by reading one of the weekly scandal sheets which will also teach you not to envy the rich and royal mired with heavy hearts in marital confusions. Or find a tabloid that explores more personal minutiae, featuring enormous front-page headlines like, "At Eighty-Four Picasso Has All His Own Teeth." How much nearer the core of French cultural life can anyone hope to be?

Paris
KATE SIMON
1967

AND, THEY SAY, ALL YOU HAVE TO DO is talk to the people of Paris to discover that they govern themselves, that they pay no attention to their bogus government and are sufficiently adult to make up their own minds. Their attitude toward official policy is one of constant mockery. In other words, Paris advances alone towards its destiny; where the people lead no government can follow. Parisian freedom of judgement is exemplary, and so is Parisian distaste for power. Paris reads between the lines of history. It has a good nose.

Tourists in Paris
Marguerite Duras
1957

And so Paris is not merely the largest town in France, not merely the political and intellectual capital where all the smartest and most ambitious people from the provinces go to seek fame and fortune. If the origins of many of the Parisians lie in *La France Profonde*, the origins of the French identity nonetheless lie in Paris. *Le tout Paris* in this sense means something more than the gathering of the small number of people in town who count most socially, though of course it does mean that as well. It also suggests that to be Parisian is to have an identity that transcends social class, economic distinction; it is to belong to a world apart, to an intellectual and moral category, not of class, race, or gender, but of a qualitative difference from the rest, an essential worldliness, a heightened expectation—as F. Scott Fitzgerald put it in a different context—of the possibilities of life.

Many people, foreigners who belonged to Paris and Parisians exiled from it, put it their own way. Rainer Maria Rilke, the German poet, identified Paris as the place where the *élan vital*, Bergson's phrase for the life force, is stronger than elsewhere. "*Élan vital*," Rilke asked, "is it life? No. Life is calm, vast, simple. It is the desire to live in haste, in pursuit; it is the impatience to possess all of life right away, right there. Paris is full of this desire; that is why it is so close to death." Victor Hugo, the great novelist and poet, exiled for many years of his life, meant the same thing when he wrote: "Ever since historic times, there has always been on the earth what we call the City. . . . We have needed the city that thinks. . . . We have needed the city where everybody is citizen. . . . Jerusalem unleashes the True. Athens the Beautiful; Rome the Great. Paris is the sum of all three of these great cities."

Fragile Glory
RICHARD BERNSTEIN
1990

M<small>Y FLIGHT HAD BEEN DICTATED</small> by my hope that I could find myself in a place where I would be treated more humanely than my society had treated me at home, where my risks would be more personal, and my fate less austerely sealed. And Paris had done this for me by leaving me completely alone. I lived in Paris for a long time without making a single French friend, and even longer before I saw the inside of a French home. This did not really upset me, either, for Henry James had been there before me and had had the generosity to clue me in. Furthermore, for a black boy who had grown up on welfare and the chicken-shit goodwill of American liberals, this total indifference came as a total relief and even as a mark of respect. If I could make it, I could make it— so much the better. And if I couldn't, I couldn't—so much the worse. I didn't want any help, and the French certainly didn't give me any They let me do it myself and for that reason, even knowing what I know, and unromantic as I am, there will always be a kind of love story between myself and that odd, unpredictable collection of bourgeois chauvinists who call themselves la France.

No Name in the Street
JAMES BALDWIN
1972

Almost simultaneously with the publisher's cocktail party and the publication of [*The Group,*] [Mary] McCarthy scorched Paris in her special television program for the British BBC, and echoing waves of it reached France. ("No," says Mlle Delattre, "it neither surprised us, nor bothered us. She always says what she thinks and expects it from the people she talks to.") Opening with the Wests' Montparnasse apartment, it continued with Miss McCarthy's other views of Paris: an empty Maxim's, a full cemetery, widows in black, backstage in a fashion house, bad taste in a department store, all background for her observations:

"Paris *is* a city of youth and love. But youth and love here are as short, it almost seems, as the mating season of birds."

"The virago is more prevalent than the siren. This business of Frenchwomen being so feminine. It seems to me that compared with Englishwomen, they are so masculine, even compared to aggressive American women, who, God knows, are the most sexless creatures in the world."

"The bedrock Parisian trait is probably resistance to change. This trait, almost animal, explains all the others: xenophobia, rigid adherence to rules, suspicion, even stinginess."

"Hemingway may have imagined that to his concierge he was 'Hemingway'—that public myth—but he wasn't, I'm sure. To his concierge, he was the monsieur who left some trunks in the cellar."

"Paris, the physical city, is beautiful, in its architecture and vistas, squares and gardens, its sky and filtered light. Paris is not false. It does not pretend. It does not ingratiate."

The People of Paris
Joseph Barry
1966

MEANS OF TRANSPORT

B Y HALF-PAST EIGHT Paris is a terrible place for walking. There's too much traffic. A blue haze of uncombusted diesel hangs over every boulevard. I know Baron Haussmann made Paris a grand place to look at, but the man had no concept of traffic flow. At the Arc de Triomphe alone thirteen roads come together. Can you imagine that? I mean to say, here you have a city with the world's most pathologically aggressive drivers—drivers who in other circumstances would be given injections of thorazine from syringes the size of bicycle pumps and confined to their beds with leather straps—and you give them an open space where they can all try to go in any of thirteen directions at once. Is that asking for trouble or what?

Paris
BILL BRYSON
1991

T HERE ARE SEVERAL WAYS of leaving Paris by motor without touching the fringe of what, were it like other cities, would be called its slums. Going, for instance, southward or south-westward, one may emerge from the alleys of the Bois near the Pont de Suresnes and, crossing the river, pass through the park of Saint-Cloud to Versailles, or through the suburbs of Rueil and Le Vésinet to the forest of Saint-Germain.

These miraculous escapes from the toils of a great city give one a clearer impression of the breadth with which it is planned, and of the civic order and elegance pervading its whole system; yet for that very reason there is perhaps more interest in a slow progress through one of the great industrial quarters such as must be crossed to reach the country lying to the north-east of Paris.

To start on a bright spring morning from the Place du Palais Bourbon, and follow the tide of traffic along the quays of the left bank, passing the splendid masses of the Louvre and Notre-Dame, the Conciergerie and the Sainte-Chapelle; to skirt the blossoming borders of the Jardin des Plantes, and cross the Seine at the Pont d'Austerlitz, getting a long glimpse down its silver reaches till they divide to envelope the Cité; and then to enter by the Boulevard Diderot on the long stretch of the Avenue Daumesnil, which leads straight to the Porte Dorée of Vincennes—to follow this route at the leisurely pace necessitated by the dense flow of traffic, is to get a memorable idea of the large way in which Paris deals with some of her municipal problems.

The Avenue Daumesnil, in particular, with its interminable warehouses and cheap shops and *guingettes,* would anywhere else be the prey of grime and sordidness. Instead, it is spacious, clean, and prosaic only by contrast to the elegance of the thoroughfares preceeding it; and at the Porte Dorée it gives one over to the charming alleys of a park as well-tended and far more beautiful than the Bois de Boulogne—a park offering the luxury of its romantic lawns and lakes for the sole delectation of the packed industrial quarters that surround it.

A Motor-Flight Through France
EDITH WHARTON
1908

THE MÉTRO SEEMED VERY EMPTY to me then, especially in comparison with the time when, sick and alone, I had ridden out to the races. Even apart from the number of passengers, the fact that it was Sunday influenced the way the Métro looked. The dark colour of the steel sides of the carriages predominated. The conductors did their work—opening and closing carriage doors and swinging themselves in and out between times—in a Sunday-afternoon manner. Everyone walked the long distances between branch connexions in leisurely fashion. The unnatural indifference with which passengers submit to a ride in the Métro was more noticeable. People seemed to face the door, or get off at unfamiliar stations far from the Opéra, as the impulse moved them. In spite of the electric lights you can definitely see the changing light of day in the stations; you notice it immediately after you've walked down, the afternoon light particularly, just before it gets dark. Arrival at the empty terminal of Porte Dauphine, a lot of tubes became visible, view into the loop where the trains make the curve they are permitted after their long trip in a straight line. Going through railway tunnels is much worse; in the Métro there isn't that feeling of oppression which a railway passenger has under the weight—though held in check—of mountains. Then, too, you aren't far off somewhere, away from people; it is rather an urban contrivance, like water pipes, for example. Tiny offices, most of them deserted, with telephones and bell systems, control the traffic. Max liked to look into them. The first time in my life I rode the Métro, from Montmartre to the main boulevards, the noise was horrible. Otherwise it hasn't been bad, even intensifies the calm, pleasant sense of speed. Métro system does away with speech; you don't have to speak either when you pay, or when you get in and out. Because it is so easy to understand, the Métro is a frail and hopeful stranger's best chance to think that he has quickly and correctly, at the first attempt, penetrated the essence of Paris.

The Diaries of Franz Kafka
FRANZ KAFKA
1911

IN PARIS THE PUBLIC TRANSPORTATION SYSTEM does not bear a vernacular name, it is not the "Underground" or the "Subway" or the

"Unterbahn": it is the Métro, the Métropolitain. A word as Greek as the word cosmopolitan. In fact, the system could easily have been called the Cosmos, since the names of its stations pretend to encompass the entirety of human history, defining as they do a mental geography that contains battlefields, poets, entire nations, capital cities, revolutionaries, animals and scientists. A lithe and elastic cosmopolitanism shines through the city in the names of its Métro stations, all of which share in the dream of the Universal City.

The Métro is above all a system of names, names which are a thousand times more secretive than the places they supposedly denote. Filles du Calvaire, Bel-Air, Crimée, Danube, Pyramides, Campo-Formio, Botzaris, Croix-de-Chavaux, Jasmin, Ourcq . . . the mercurial names of the Métro, with the exoticism of the names of extinct birds and buried cities.

Paris Dreambook
Lawrence Osborne
1990

It is a concert hall whose acoustics are incredible but whose audience is hard to hold. It is also a bazaar, a den of thieves, an unofficial social agency, a flower shop, a public urinal, a bedding place for the homeless, an asylum for the harmlessly deranged, a fashion show, a political stage, a stink, a rush of wind.

Last, and almost incidentally, it is a means of transport, the system of hidden arteries through which the city's lifeblood flows. It is the Paris métro.

A Paris Notebook
C. W. Gusewelle
1985

PRESENCE OF THE PAST

In the evening I strolled the eighteen miles to the Ile de la Cité and Notre-Dame, through the sort of neighborhoods where swarthy men in striped Breton shirts lean against lampposts cleaning their teeth with flick knives and spit between your legs as you pass. But it was a lovely March evening, with just the faintest tang of spring in the air, and once I stumbled onto the Seine, at the Pont de Sully, I was met with perfection. There facing me was the Ile St-Louis, glowing softly and floating on the river like a vision, a medieval hamlet magically preserved in the midst of a modern city. I crossed the bridge and wandered up and down its shuttered streets, half expecting to find chickens wandering in the road and peasants pushing carts loaded with plague victims, but what I found instead were tiny, swish restaurants and appealing apartments in old buildings.

Paris
BILL BRYSON
1991

One winter day in 1932, I got the urge to climb to the top of Notre-Dame at night.

"The concierge is on the second floor," they told me at the entrance. So I climbed up—200 steps—and between two groups of tourists, I confronted the woman who watched over Notre-Dame.

"Climb up here at night, sir? It's unheard of! It's out of the question. We're a national museum, just like the Louvre. And we close at five!"

I discreetly slipped her a bill.

"I shouldn't let you, sir! It's wrong! Even though I am very badly paid . . . and I have heart trouble, and I'm short of breath . . . Imagine! Two hundred steps every time I come up, and such steps! I was young once, not so fat, and I

47

climbed up here twice a day. Now I come up in the morning and bring my lunch, and I don't go back until evening. . . . Coming up here twice in one day will be hard on me, very hard. But you're generous, and you love Notre-Dame! I'll do it for you . . . a favor I've never done for anyone else . . . Only promise me not to use any light, not even a match. We're right across from the Préfecture de Police. The slightest glimmer would be suspicious. I could lose my job over it. . . ."

I reassure her. Taking advantage of a lull while the tourists moved off, the capacious woman continued in a low voice: "Look." With her plump finger, she indicated a particular place down in the square. "You see the third lamppost on the right? Be there at ten tonight. I don't want you to come looking for me in the concierge's loge."

I was under the lamppost on the stroke of ten, and through the November mist, I saw a voluminous silhouette emerge from the Rue du Cloître-Notre-Dame and come toward me.

"Follow me," the concierge whispered in a muffled voice.

We were like conspirators in a Victor Hugo novel. She carried a bunch of keys, and with them she opened the heavy door.

We climbed the spiral staircase. It was totally dark; the climb lasted an eternity. At last, we reached the open platform. Completely out of breath, my accomplice collapsed into her chair. Impatient, enraptured, I ran beside the balustrade. It was more beautiful than I had imagined! The dark, indefinable shapes were black as night, the fog over Paris was milk white! Scarcely discernible, the Hôtel-Dieu, the Tour Saint-Jacques, the Quartier latin, the Sorbonne, were luminous and somber shapes . . . Paris was ageless, bodiless . . . Present and past, history and legend, intermingled. Atop this cathedral, I expected to meet Quasimodo the bell-ringer around some corner, and later, upon descending into the city, I would certainly pass Verlaine and François Villon, the Marquis de Sade, Gérard de Nerval, Restif de la Bretonne.

"It's marvelous, marvelous," I kept exclaiming to myself.

"Isn't it, sir?" the fat woman replied, brimming with pride at being the concierge of Notre-Dame. "You don't see that anywhere else . . . We're at the heart of Paris . . . It beats the Eiffel Tower, doesn't it?"

But I had to get to the very top.

"Climb on up if you want, sir. I'll stay here; I can't go any farther . . . I trust you. Go on. You won't steal the towers of Notre-Dame."

So up I climbed, still in complete darkness. I mounted the 378 steps. Coming out at the top, I saw behind the cathedral's spire the Seine glittering like a curved sword. Suddenly my foot brushed against something soft. I bent down, and beneath my fingers, numb from the cold of that November night, I felt the feathers of a dead pigeon. A dead pigeon, still warm.

The Secret Paris of the 30's
BRASSAÏ
1932

EVERYTHING I SAW—the chestnut trees scattering their leaves along the walks, the wide bridges clustered with bookstalls at either end, the medieval town of Ile de la Cité over which Notre-Dame raised its ponderous, Gothic stones—evoked that strange pang which even first-time visitors to Paris recognize, with some astonishment, as *nostalgia*. A buried memory seems to stab at your consciousness in Paris, and you follow in the steps of an elusive phantom of *déjà vu*, but never quite catch up. So deeply embedded in the world's dream of freedom, youth, art, and pleasure has this city become, that the feeling that the stranger in Paris is a feeling of *return*. Perhaps one misses friends so keenly there because all of one's senses are pitched to such a keen note of receptivity, and one vibrates with an awareness that one longs to share.

A Wake in the Streets of Paris
JOHN CLELLON HOLMES
1987

PARIS HAS NEVER BEEN MORE BEAUTIFUL. Emptied, in part, of its civilian population, it looks much larger. It is recovering the harmonious proportions of an uncongested city. The scale of its squares is easily visible. Very old arteries, ordinarily filled with commercial traffic, become narrow byways again, destined for pedestrians. An ancient building finds itself surrounded once more by the space its architect originally planned. . . . In the nighttime quiet, Paris again hears sounds it has forgotten, the bells of the Angélus and the early Mass; and, before daybreak, the hoarse bellowing of a river barge crosses a vast silence of water and gardens and colonnades, of the Seine and the Tuileries, the Louvre, the Carrousel, and the Palais-Royal, to reach me in my sleep.

From a radio broadcast over Paris Mondial
COLETTE
1939

PICTURESQUENESS! The place was steeped in it. It was not an ordinary apartment, but an artist's studio, with one wall almost all glass, an authentic artist's skylight even though it faced west, not north. From it I looked over the rooftops of Paris with, in the foreground, the perfectly proportioned old stone tower of St-Germain-des-Prés and, in the background, the Eiffel Tower. The view from the bedroom window was even better. It commanded one of the oldest parts of Paris, whose roofs in 1927 still looked like those of a village, covered with red tiles and bristling with chimneys, each enclosing a tight bundle of pale red tubes, one for each fireplace. The houses were clustered around narrow winding medieval streets. The backdrop was the cathedral of Notre-Dame.

Even the address sounded picturesque—3, rue de l'Ancienne-Comédie. The Comédie-Française had been situated here, on the other side of the street, for about a century starting in 1689. In earlier times the rue de l'Ancienne-Comédie, not yet under that name, and perhaps with no name at all, had been nothing but a path beaten out by the wooden shoes of peasants rounding the wall built there in 1209 by Philip Augustus; today it runs toward the Seine from the boulevard St-Michel. Five doors down on my side of the street, at no. 13, was its most famous establishment after the Comédie, or even including it, for it was older—the Café Procope, where, in 1670, a Sicilian named Francesco Procopio del Cotillo opened a café and introduced the Parisian public to Coffee, an exotic import from Italy. It was perhaps also the first place in Paris to serve sherbert. The café is operating still, with plaques on some of its chairs indicating the spots that the management is willing you should think were regularly occupied by Voltaire, Diderot, Danton, Balzac, and other notables during its three-hundred-year history.

3, rue de l'Ancienne-Comédie
WAVERLEY ROOT
1987

Dear Don,

I am sitting at a small wooden table in the corner of our tiny and yet curiously comfortable room at the Hôtel Récamier. It is truly a jewel of a hotel in its physical arrangements, its management, and its location. The address here is 3/bis Place Saint-Sulpice; and if and when you and Jane come to Paris, I recommend that you write them a card and try to stay here. The hotel is tucked charmingly and quietly into one corner of the great square in front of Saint-Sulpice, an immense, awkward, twin-towered church, whose stones are the color of pure bees' honey in the spring sunlight. Just inside the front entrance, to the right, there are two huge frescoes by Delacroix, and to me the great one is the picture of Jacob wrestling with the angel. The church as I say seems somehow awkward, but it must have been constructed with some care, because the acoustics are totally marvelous. Marcel Dupré was the organist there for some years. Most wonderful of all, Mozart came there when he was six or seven years old and played the organ. And for Marie-Antoinette, for heaven's sake.

From a letter sent to Donald Hall
JAMES WRIGHT
1979

Other cities modestly hid their public urinals below the ground. Paris, like the good Latin city it is, erected them out in the open, in public squares, on the streets. In the thirties, there were more than 1,300 of them. These miniature shelters in various styles—round or square, graceful, clumsy, sometimes baroque, topped off with one or more lamps—often resembled sentry boxes or advertising kiosks, even pagodas. Their genealogy goes back to the first century of our era, to the days of Emperor Vespasian, the first benefactor to offer amphoras to the Romans for use as urinals.

Most of the *pissotières* in Paris date from around 1900. There has been great argument as to their aesthetic value, and even their utility. Are they not exclusively and selfishly reserved for the use of men? But like the Morris Columns and the Wallace Fountains, like the newspaper kiosks, they have become familiar sights in the Parisian urban landscape. Henry Miller spoke of them frequently, with tears in his eyes. He praised the French for having almost always known just how to pick the best spot on which to erect one. He gives lyrical descriptions of these places, "where the water gurgles melodiously." "There are," he wrote, "some urinals that I go out of my way to visit, like the old, dilapidated one in front of the school for the deaf-mutes on the corner of the Rue Saint-Jacques and the Rue Abbé-de-l'Epée."

At nightfall, the urinal lamps lit up with the streetlamps. These tiny chapels served an odd religion. They were public conveniences, but also meeting grounds and cruising areas for homosexuals, particularly the round urinals with three stalls, whose circular layout allowed for direct contact. Darkness was also part of the attraction. "Darkness," Proust wrote, "has the effect of eliminating the first stage of pleasure and of allowing us to enter straightaway into a world of caresses at which we usually arrive only after some time has passed . . . In the darkness, all of the old habits fall away, hands, lips, bodies can act immediately." And Proust mentions this "immediate response of the body which does not withdraw, which approaches (and) gives us an unprejudiced notion of the person we silently address, full of vice, a notion that provides us the additional pleasure in having succeeded in tasting the fruit without having desired it with our eyes, and without having asked permission." In those days, this somber ballet, the comings and goings of the inverts, went on through the night. Neither the smell nor the dirt of these places repulsed the devotees of

Greek love. On the contrary. The more malodorous the chapels, the more popular they became.

The vice squad would turn up occasionally, and many famous names in the arts and literature, or in high society, fell into its net. Proust, who was the first to dare to reveal in his novel the underside of Sodom and Gomorrah—with more irony than charity—did not leave out the *vespasiennes.* Of course, the Baron de Charlus was an assiduous visitor. "The Baron de Charlus must have caught a disease," the Duc de Guermantes's valet naively tells him, "to stand about as long as he does in the *pistière.* I saw him go into the *pistière* in the Rue de Bourgogne. When I came back from Neuilly over an hour later, I saw his yellow trousers, in the same *pistière,* in the same place, in the middle stall where he always goes so that people shan't see him" (*The Captive*). Considered an outrage to public decency, such a misdemeanor could cost as much as from two months to three years in prison and a fine of from 500 to 4,500 francs. Despite this risk, despite the sentence, the inverts faithfully patronized their tearooms, their "cups," as the urinals were called, and the nocturnal ballet continued with renewed vigor.

To put a stop to such practices, the Paris Municipal Council moved a few years back to get rid of all of them, and they began with the tearooms with three communicating stalls. So the habitués, on a certain evening, would walk up and find nothing but an empty spot where their favorite chapel had once stood. From 1,300 the number of *pissotières* fell gradually to 350, and soon they will all be gone. Having become historical monuments, like the art nouveau subway entrances that are already being collected, will they be installed in museums and in collections in the New World? And won't France be sorry one day to have taken so little care to preserve them? "For," as Henry Miller wrote, "how can a Frenchman know that one of the first things that strikes the eye of a newly arrived American, and which moves him and warms his guts, is the omnipresent urinal?"

The Secret Paris of the 30's
BRASSAÏ
1930's

AT THE VICTOR HUGO MUSEUM. In the room with the four-poster bed, in a glass case at the foot of the bed, there is a death mask of the old madman, complete with a beard that might be the work of Bernini. I saw, leaning over the case, the charming face of a young man with black hair and brown cheeks. Hugo would have adored the contrast. Outside in the place des Vosges they were felling the elms. It was almost as if they were removing all trace of thousands of rendez-vous, some tender, some cruel—because here people were just as likely to have it out with weapons as with madrigals.

Paris
JULIAN GREEN
1992

AFTER MY FIRST WEEK IN PARIS I have given up on monuments. I read authors I have not read since high school and college—Balzac, Gide, Stendhal, Beckett, Hemingway, Sartre. In Balzac's *Père Goriot*, the impecunious law student, Eugène, goes to call on a great lady whose home is enclosed within a courtyard. On his way, horses have splattered his shabby boots; the toes are muddy. Looking up at the lady's windows and down on his shabby boots, Eugène feels the shame of his poverty, his lack of place in Parisian life. From the outside, where Eugène stands, this life looks marvelous to him, and also unapproachable. He wants in. He longs for a carriage, for five francs for a cab that will drive him into this courtyard.

I look into these courtyards. Narrow streetside doors, hung with signs that read, "Cour Privée," block a passerby's access. But I look. The courtyard's size is a surprise, three and four stories up, and as many as six doors opening into living quarters. The yards themselves are cobbled stone. The smell is of drains, of heat on the broad humped stones and grayed walls, of moss and lichen, of clay flowerpots that have just been watered. White lace curtains cover the windows. Like Eugène, I feel that Paris life looks wonderful. I want in.

A Postcard From Paris
JUDITH MOORE
1984

THE APARTMENT THAT TURNED UP was rather crowded for the three of us: my wife, our eleven-year-old daughter, and myself. It constituted most of the cement-floored *rez-de-chaussée* of a small and shored-up building which dated from the fifteenth century, and indeed had been condemned to be torn down almost forty years before. It faced toward a pleasant courtyard and away from the street, which was aptly named—as I was to realize—for an eighteenth-century grammarian, the Abbé Lhomond. One direction led there from official Paris: the *grandes écoles*, the Panthéon, the University. The other dipped down into the winding market of the Rue Mouffetard, and into the very oldest part of the city, with its Roman arena and other ruins. Across our corner ran the Rue du Pot-de-Fer, where the language heard was Arabic. Near the head of the street was the École Normale, and at that conjunction two *clochards* slept regularly over a Métro grating. Our distinguished neighbor, when we got to know him, proved to be a proud and knowledgeable guide to his *quartier.* Here if anywhere was the ancient Lutetia, he liked to point out, as well as the medieval Latin Quarter that harbored François Villon. Jean Valjean had once escaped from the Inspector Javert by climbing over the convent wall across the street, and a stone's throw away was the *pension* where Eugène de Rastignac had met the Père Goriot.

34 Rue Lhomond: Francis Ponge
HARRY LEVIN
1974

My apartment on Rue des Écouffes was furnished with imitation Empire lamps and an Oriental rug worn to a kind of mud color. There was an enameled gas heater of florid design. The wallpaper, of tint multicolored flowers, had long since faded to something like late autumn. It was a place out of another century. Zola and Balzac prowled in its faded decor. In winter, the smoke from dozens of chimneys rose like skywriting from the adjoining buildings. My bed sagged in the middle, that's where Claire and I ended up in the morning, rolled into the gulch of the old feather mattress.

Departures
PAUL ZWEIG
1986

We strolled around the Fauchon side of the Madeleine and then down the Rue Royale to the Tuileries. In the central path the African vendors tried to sell their multicolored plastic birds. They wound up the bands on the birds' insides and sent them off on demented flights through the trees. Either they would attract passing children or be trodden on for a forced sale.

We walked across the park as far as the balcony looking over the river. Floating across on the far bank, the decks of Deligny were still covered with people. I would miss my swim now. We walked back toward the Rivoli gate. In the sand along the wall groups of men were still playing *pétanque*. We watched them measuring up the small wooden ball and then throwing their metal balls toward it. They landed with a thud and raised dust. Near the players the small donkeys were being tethered together for their walk to the stables after all the rides of the day. We crossed the Rue de Rivoli to the arcades and walked up the Rue de Castiglione. I gave her my tour. I showed her the building where Chopin let out his last breath and told her about all the cannons from the Battle of Austerlitz that Napoléon had melted down into the Vendôme column.

An Available Man
PATRIC KUH
1990

W<small>E ABANDONED THE SEARCH</small>, standing in front of a bar called King Kong, where Richard may have had breakfast in a former life of the establishment twenty years before and Rilke fifty years before that. The morning had begun to warm up, and the streets filled with people. Like many other young artists at the turn of the century, Rilke was drawn to Paris, and there, under the tutelage of Rodin, he began to be a great writer in the poems of *Neue Gedichte*, but he didn't altogether like the city, either its poverty or its glamour, both of which shocked at first and saddened him later. It was hard, watching the street come alive with shopkeepers, students in long scarves, professors in sleek jackets solemnly lecturing companions of the previous night who walked shivering beside them, shoppers already out and armed with that French look of fanatic skepticism, not to set beside the scene the annihilating glimpse of the city in the Fifth Elegy:

> Squares, oh square in Paris, infinite showplace
>
> where the milliner Madame Lamort
>
> twists and winds the restless paths of the earth,
>
> those endless ribbons, and, from them, designs
>
> new bows, frills, flowers, ruffles, artificial fruits—, all
>
> falsely colored,—for the cheap
>
> winter bonnets of Fate.

Looking for Rilke
ROBERT HASS
1984

For the rest (I must rectify) it is not so, Paris could not have altered essentially. The conditions of its greatness seem to be so basic and constant that again and again something extreme and unsurpassable seems to emerge from them as from the root, and I recognize continually what caused me bliss and dismay years ago, and in the face of it am experiencing the being no less overpowered. At most the current that flows over these essentials has become thicker, more ruthless, more hurried (but beneath it the outlasting nature of this incomparable city is conserving itself all the more secretly). If, for hours now and then, I have to grant the change, it is because this time I myself occasionally drift along in this superficial current—, but how gladly I sever myself from it, to belong to the other Paris that is still the Paris of Villon or Charles-Louis Philippe, the Paris of Gérard de Nerval and Baudelaire, that complete Paris which, in the infinite spirituality of its space, comes into all its heritage and includes in itself all vibrations: the only city that could become a

landscape of life and death beneath the exhaustless affirmation of its magnani-
mous and weightless skies.

From a letter sent to Anton Kippenberg
RAINER MARIA RILKE
1925

YOU KNOW, you and the *babbo* always said that I was an egalitarian.
That used to embarrass me, but it's true. I've got this bug about equality. And
now I'm in the place where the whole thing started, where you see *Liberté, Égal-
ité, Fraternité* frowning at you in gold letters from the faces of public buildings.
They even have it on the fronts of *churches,* sometimes stenciled and sometimes
cut right into the stone. As though some kid had gone wild with some rubber
stamp that it got for its birthday. The handwriting on the wall, only it's printed
in big Roman letters. This must go back to the Revolution, when churches were
turned into powder-magazines or temples of Reason or Glory. Funny that in all
these years nobody erased it; I wonder if the Germans tried during the
Occupation. Out, damned spot. You would think the guidebooks would have a
word to say about this revolutionary slogan, which hits every tourist in the eye,
but they pass it over in silence, just as if it was of those obscene graffiti you see
in the Métro. OAS or A BAS LES JUIFS.

Birds of America
MARY McCARTHY
1965

FROM 1900 TO 1930, Paris did change a lot. They always told me
that America changed but it really did not change as much as Paris did in those
years that is the Paris that one can see, but then there is no remembering what
it looked like before and even no remembering what it looks like now.

We none of us lived in old parts of Paris then. We lived in the rue de Fleurus just a hundred year old quarter, a great many of us lived around there and on the boulevard Raspail which was not even cut through then and when it was cut through all the rats and animals came underneath our house and we had to have one of the vermin catchers of Paris come and clean us out, I wonder if they exist any more now, they have disappeared along with the horses and enormous wagons that used to clean out the sewers under the houses that were not in the new sewerage system, now even the oldest houses are in the new system. It is nice in France they adapt themselves to everything slowly they change completely but all the time they know that they are as they were.

Paris France
Gertrude Stein
1940

SEASONS, RAIN, LIGHT

Paris is always beautiful, even during the months when we forsake it. To make this discovery we have to come back to it in October, when river and stone are steeped in the splendour of the early autumn sun.

A storm had swept over the city that morning and large drops of warm rain had washed the grey quays. The trees bending towards the Seine were laden with drops from the purple sky, and the dark ivy carpeting the base of Notre-Dame gleamed as if it had been newly polished.

I went right along the old quays purposely walking slowly so as to savour the purity of the rain-washed air, and the mixed smells of vegetation and tar. This corner of Paris should be the preserve of painters and poets, for this is where the city's essence can best be understood.

In the Heart of Paris
Yvonne de Bremond d'Ars
1957

Four, five, six drops of water. Some people, anxious about their straw hats, raise their noses. Description of a storm in Paris. In summer. The timid take to their heels; others raise the collars of their jackets, which gives them an air of bravado. It begins to smell of mud. Many people prudently look for shelter, and when the rain is at its height, all that can be seen are blackish groups, clustered around doorways, like mussels around the pile of a pier.

The Bark Tree
Raymond Queneau
1933

Dear Franz,

It is raining in Paris this morning. I have been working at this desk for the past couple of hours, as I've done every morning for days, and I feel plumb tuckered out. Not really, but sort of. The Higgins's apartment is on the ninth floor, and the Dr.'s study has a tiny window in the wall just to my right. I can lean forward slightly and see all the way across the city to the domes of the church of Sacré-Coeur in Montmartre, where, not so terribly long ago, those wonderful poets Max Jacob and Francis Carco used to meet for lunch. Franz, old man, Paris is one of the cities I would love to share with you some time. Of all the cities it has the most beautiful varied light. The domes of Sacré-Coeur look like pearl-onions floating in the mist.

From a letter sent to Franz Wright
JAMES WRIGHT
1979

April 7

Last fall Virgil Thomson and I, featured stars on the same concert, were seated together in the front row of a small auditorium. Virgil, so deaf now as to find all music pointless and unable to gauge the force of his own voice, remains nevertheless the least foolish man around. The lights dimmed as we chatted of this and that, and I asked him where to stay in Paris. "Hôtel du Quai Voltaire is the only place," said Virgil—whereupon a lady in taupe chiffon emerged onto the stage to play his Violin Sonata. Virgil dropped off. During a hush after the first movement, as the player retuned her fiddle, Virgil awoke and piped resonantly: "But you can't bring anyone up to your room."

April 8

It's raining. It began again before dawn, continued vehemently all day so that one wondered at nature's stamina (who would have thought the old sky had so much blood in it!), and now has subsided to a fevered seeping which lends to the boulevards an ashy hemorrhaged aspect, not at all unpleasant. Alone in the Café Cyrano. Though it's only six o'clock the street looks like midnight. Sixteen years ago I'd have felt like a Jean Rhys heroine, but in the interim I've had not a drop of alcohol. Snuggly before me sits not a *coup de rouge* or three but a foaming cup of hot chocolate, a brioche, and a jar of hard butter. The solitude is exquisite. Anxious forms beneath umbrellas converge outside like rioting mushrooms toward the Métro, but in here a central stove hisses and I think about Piaf and Simenon and don't feel morose at all, as I write these notes on the zinc table.

The Nantucket Diary of Ned Rorem
NED ROREM
1984

DARLING

I went to Chartier to lunch and had a macquereau grillé et épinards à la crème. It was very strange to be there alone—I felt that I was a tiny little girl standing on a chair looking into an aquarium. It was not a sad feeling, only strange and a bit 'femme seulish'—As I came out it began to snow. A wind like a carving knife cut through the streets—and everybody began to run—so did I into a café and there I sat and drank a cup of hot black coffee. Then for the first time I felt in Paris. It was a little café & hideous—with a black marble top to the counter garni with lozenges of white and orange. Chauffeurs and their wives & fat men with immense photographic apparatus sat in it—and a white fox terrier bitch—thin and eager ran among the tables. Against the window beat a dirty French flag, fraying out in the wind and then flapping on the glass. Does black coffee make you drunk—do you think? I felt quite enivrée (Oh Jack I *won't* do this. It's like George Moore. Don't be cross) and could have sat there years, smoking & sipping and thinking and watching the flakes of snow.

From a letter to John Middleton Murry
KATHERINE MANSFIELD
1915

I MAKE A TRIP TO EACH CLOCK IN THE APARTMENT:
some hands point histrionically one way
and some point others, from the ignorant faces.
Time is an Étoile; the hours diverge
so much that days are journeys round the suburbs,
circles surrounding stars, overlapping circles.
The short, half-tone scale of winter weathers
is a spread pigeon's wing.
Winter lives under a pigeon's wing, a dead wing with damp
    feathers.

Look down into the courtyard. All the houses
are built that way, with ornamental urns
set on the mansard roof-tops where the pigeons
take their walks. It is like introspection
to stare inside, or retrospection,
a star inside a rectangle, a recollection:

this hollow square could easily have been there.
—The childish snow-forts, built in flashier winters,
could have reached these proportions and been houses;
the mighty snow-forts, four, five, stories high,
withstanding spring as sand-forts do the tide,
their walls, their shape, could not dissolve and die,
only be overlapping in a strong chain, turned to stone,
and grayed and yellowed now like these.

Where is the ammunition, the piled-up balls
with the star-splintered hearts of ice?
This sky is no carrier-warrior-pigeon
escaping endless intersecting circles.
It is a dead one, or the sky from which a dead one fell.
The urns have caught his ashes or his feathers.
When did the star dissolve, or was it captured
by the sequence of squares and squares and circles, circles?
Can the clocks say; is it there below,
about to tumble in snow?

Paris, 7 A.M.
ELIZABETH BISHOP
1946

Paris is so very beautiful, particularly in the dark winter
light. I'm surprised you don't love it more. I still love Africa best I guess, but
there one must shut one's eyes against a great many things too. Here there is the
Right Bank, and there the Villes Nouvelles, the buses, and the European shoes.

You know what I mean. To cross the river never ceases to excite me. I went to see *Phèdre* at the Comédie-Française with Nora. I am wildly excited about it. The only thing I have enjoyed thoroughly in years. I have never heard French *grand théâtre* before. I don't know how good the players were, but one must be good to do Racine at all. I shall go now as often as possible.

From a letter sent to Paul Bowles
JANE BOWLES
1950

AFTER I RETURNED TO PARIS, I spent my days alone reading and writing, and in fair weather I'd eat a sandwich on the quay. That January the Seine overflowed and flooded the highway on the Right Bank. Seagulls flew upstream and wheeled above the turbulent river, crying, as though mistaking Notre-Dame for Mont-St-Michel. The floodlights trained on the church's facade projected ghostly shadows of the two square towers up into the foggy night sky, as though spirits were doing axonometric drawings of a cathedral I had always thought of as malign. The gargoyles were supposed to ward off evil, but to me they looked like dogs straining to leap away from the devil comfortably lodged within.

Skinned Alive
EDMUND WHITE
1989

FIRST FAINT IMPRESSION OF URBAN AUTUMN. There are memories which are brought into play by certain sounds, smells or changes in temperature; like those tunes which recur in the mind at a given time of year. With the sweeping up of the dead leaves in the square, the first misty morning, the first yellowing of the planes, I remember Paris and the old excitement of looking for autumn lodgings in an hotel. Streets round the Rue de l'Université, Rue Jacob, Rue de Bourgogne and Rue de Beaune, with their hotel signs and hall-ways where the concierge sits walled in by steamer trunks. A stuffy salon full of novels by Edith Wharton, the purple wall-paper which we will grow to hate as we lie in bed with grippe, the chintz screen round the bidet, the tall grey paneling with a cupboard four inches deep.

The Unquiet Grave
Cyril Connolly
1944

I DAWDLED OVER MY WORK IN PARIS. It was very agreeable in the springtime, with chestnuts in the Champs-Élysées in bloom and the light in the streets so gay. There was pleasure in the air, a light transitory pleasure, sensual without grossness, that made your step more springy and your intelligence more alert. I was happy in the various company of my friends and, my heart filled with amiable memories of the past, I regained in spirit at least something of the glow of youth. I thought I should be a fool to allow work to interfere with a delight in the passing moment that I might never enjoy again so fully.

The Razor's Edge
W. Somerset Maugham
1943

IN PARIS IN SPRING the chestnut trees bloom: the first on the Boulevard Pasteur where the subway emerges from underground and heated air rises in waves to the trees. Every autumn the leaves of the Champs-Élysées, before falling, turn a dark brown, the colour of a cigar. In summer there are several days when the sun sits in the center of the Arc de Triomphe on the Étoile, if you look from the Place de la Concorde. The gardens of the Tuileries are the most beautiful in Paris because they are a part of the ensemble, and anyone who stands and looks at the red sun pouring onto the stone of the Arc on the Étoile also becomes part of the ensemble, as in front of 'Aristotle Contemplating the Bust of Homer' you 'contemplate' Rembrandt and feel alive. There are no winters, properly speaking, in Paris: rain falls, rustles, bangs, whispers at the window and on the roofs, one day, two, three. In January there is suddenly a day—towards the end of the month—when all shines and pours out warmly; the sky is blue, people sit on the terraces of cafés without coats, and women in light dresses transform the city. This is like a promise. It is the first hint that all will again be cheerful, beautiful, that all around will sparkle. It is only a single day, and though everyone knows two months of awful weather are still to come, they keep silent about it.

The Italics Are Mine
NINA BERBEROVA
1992

AUGUST WAS A HOT, OPPRESSIVE MONTH, the sun beating down on sleepy streets, the cafés and restaurants nearly empty, the staircase and passages of the Hôtel du Bosphore and its fellows pervaded by an extraordinary mixture of smells. Drains, face powder, scent, garlic, drains. Above all, drains.

Quartet
JEAN RHYS
1928

JUNE. LUXEMBOURG GARDENS

A Sunday morning full of wind and sunlight. Over the large pool the wind splatters the waters of the fountain; the tiny sailboats on the windswept water and the swallows around the huge trees. Two youths discussing: "You who believe in human dignity."

Notebooks 1942–1951
ALBERT CAMUS
1943

SO IT'S YOUR LAST DAY WITH ADOLPHE." Anna and I were walking in the late morning sunshine. We stopped on the Pont d'Iéna to watch the sun dancing on the water. "It's like a Bach fugue," she went on, "the light— thesis, antithesis . . . everything finding its place in a counterpane of light. What a pun . . . Quel beau rêve."

Burning Houses
ANDREW HARVEY
1986

WE WERE NURSING OUR APERITIFS sitting outside a café on the Champs-Élysées. Praise, compliments for the two waves beneath the Rose Descat hat. Now Hermine had fallen silent and was contemplating the red glow of her cigarette in the silky lament of the falling dusk. Paris had a scent of expensive tobacco, Paris was scented with Mitsouko; the dusk, like dawn tumbling its dreams of light before it, was moving toward us with the caress of a wood fire sinking to rest. I turned my head: Hermine was so calm beside me, so close that she belonged to me. A hive of murmurs as the cars with their open tops filed past.

La Bâtarde
VIOLETTE LEDUC
1964

At dusk by Les Invalides
a few old men play at boules,
tossing, holding
the crouch, listening for the clack
of steel on steel, strolling over, studying the ground.

Always at boules it's the creaking grace, the slow amble, the stillness,
always it's the dusk deepening,
always it's the plane trees casting down their leaves,
always it's the past blowing its terrors behind distracted eyes.

Always
it is empty cots lined up
in the darkness of rooms, where the last true men
would listen each dusk
for the high, thin, sweet clack
sounding from the home village far away.

Les Invalides
GALWAY KINNELL
1980

On the french grass, in that room on Fifth Ave., lay that woman who had never seen my own poor land. The dust and noise of Paris had fallen from her with the dress and underwear and shoes and stockings which she had just put aside to lie bathing in the sun. So too she lay in the sunlight of the man's easy attention. His eye and the sun had made day over her. She gave herself to them both for there was nothing to be told. Nothing is to be told to the

sun at noonday. A violet clump before her belly mentioned that it was spring.
A locomotive could be heard whistling beyond the hill. There was nothing to
be told. Her body was neither classic nor what it might be supposed. There she
lay and her curving torso and thighs were close upon the grass and violets.

A Matisse
WILLIAM CARLOS WILLIAMS
1921

THE THREE MUSKETEERS CAFÉ gleamed through the faltering
dusk with all its lights ablaze. A desultory crowd had assembled on the terrace
outside. Soon the luminous network of the night would be stretched above
Paris; these people were waiting for the night, listening to the band, and looking happy enough as they gathered gratefully round this first red glimmer of the
night to come.

The Age of Reason
JEAN-PAUL SARTRE
1945

F O O D

Renoir considered himself a Parisian. At that period the Esplanade of the Louvre, instead of opening on the Tuileries Gardens, was shut off by the Tuileries Palace, which was destroyed by fire under the Commune. Today this space is planted with flowers which vary with the season, but in 1845 it was lined with houses, and the Rue d'Argenteuil extended through it as far as the Seine. These houses had been built in the sixteenth century by the Valois to shelter the families of the noblemen of the Palace Guard. The broken cornices, the cracked columns and the remains of coats-of-arms bore witness to their former elegance. The original owners had long ago been replaced by people of less affluence. It was in one of these houses that my grandfather found an apartment to let, and he moved in with his family.

One wonders how successive kings could have tolerated such a seedy neighborhood under their very noses. The quarter was a perfect network of lanes and alleys which crossed each other in the most wayward fashion. The washing was hung out to dry from the windows, and the smells floating up from the kitchens indicated the different regions from which the inhabitants had come. This is easy to imagine, for the march of progress has not yet succeeded in standardizing the quality of French cooking. In Paris the steam from the casseroles still gives the passer-by a clue as to whether a Burgundian is stewing kidney beans with bacon or a Provençal is preparing a dish heavily flavoured with garlic.

Renoir, My Father
Jean Renoir
1958

One particularly gloomy evening comes to my mind. I had eaten nothing since the previous day. At that time I was in the habit of going frequently to see one of my friends who lived with his parents not very far from the Lecourbe Métro station and had noticed that, if I calculated the time of my arrival properly, they always asked me to stay to dinner.

My stomach was empty and I thought it might be a good idea to pay a polite call on them. I even took one of my manuscripts to read aloud, for I felt very kindly disposed toward Monsieur and Madame Bondy. I was almost mad with hunger and also with that feeling of indignation, resentment and mean rage which an empty stomach always stirs up in me. I planned to be passing by sheer coincidence—just when the soup would appear upon the table. When I reached the Place de la Contrescarpe, I could already smell in my imagination the delicious brew of potatoes and leeks, though I was still forty-five minutes' walk from the rue Lecourbe—I hadn't enough money to pay for a Métro ticket. My mouth was watering and there must have been a gleam of crazy concupiscence in my eyes, judging from the way such unaccompanied women as I passed gave me a wide berth and increased their pace. I was also pretty certain there would be Hungarian salami too—there always had been, on previous occasions. I don't think I ever went to a lover's tryst with so delicious a sense of anticipation.

Promise at Dawn
ROMAIN GARY
1961

YOU GOT VERY HUNGRY when you did not eat enough in Paris because all the bakery shops had such good things in the windows and people ate outside at tables on the sidewalks so that you saw and smelled the food. When you had given up journalism and were writing nothing that anyone in America would buy, explaining at home that you were lunching out with someone, the best place to go was the Luxembourg gardens where you saw and smelled nothing to eat all the way from Place de l'Observatoire to the rue de Vaugirard. There you could always go into the Luxembourg museum and all the paintings were sharpened and clearer and more beautiful if you were belly-empty, hollow-hungry. I learned to understand Cézanne much better and to see truly how he made landscapes when I was hungry.

A Moveable Feast
Ernest Hemingway
1964

We ORDERED A COUPLE OF DOZEN *escargots en pots de chambre* to begin with. These are snails baked and served, for the client's convenience, in individual earthenware crocks, instead of being forced back into shells. The snail, of course, has to be taken out of his shell to be prepared for cooking. The shell he is forced back into may not be his own. There is thus not even a sentimental justification for his reincarnation. The frankness of the service *en pot* does not improve the preparation of the snail, nor does it detract from it, but it does facilitate and accelerate his consumption. (The notion that the shell proves the snail's authenticity, like the head left on a woodcock, is invalid, as even a suburban housewife knows nowadays; you can buy a tin of snail shells in a super-market and fill them with a mixture of nutted cream cheese and chopped olives.)

Between Meals
A. J. Liebling
1959

And IN THE RUE Notre-Dame-des-Champs, where Hemingway, in his rooms above a sawmill, had produced some of his first stories and Ezra Pound used to be seen in his velvet beret coming in and out of his studio, Katherine Anne Porter occupied a *pavillon.*

Katherine Anne had a handsome tomcat named Skipper. His mistress was such a good cook that Skipper began to lose his figure. She invented a sort of Swedish system, with pulleys attached to a tree, that forced Skipper to do exercises in the garden. But Skipper was not the slim type.

One day Skipper had a narrow escape. He was sitting at the street gate observing passers-by—and his mistress came out just in time to see a woman putting him into a large basket. "But wait," she cried, "that's my cat!" In another minute it would have been too late. Many plump cats disappear in Paris; they make such nice rabbit stews.

Shakespeare and Company
Sylvia Beach
1956

Dear Moms—

Getting back to Paris was very nice: next to getting back to Mississippi will be. I have just had a magnificent dinner, 32 cents, at the 3 Musketeers—one of my regular places. The grilled leg of rabbit (I kidded the waitress about it, but I don't think it was cat) cauliflower with cheese, figs and nuts and a glass of wine. The restaurant is kind of a club—a small place where you see the same people every night: a quiet young French couple, a lady who wears a colored handkerchief around her neck and a man's cap, like a bandit, an old Englishman who has lived in Paris for 50 years, a young American photographer and myself.

From a letter sent to his mother
William Faulkner
1925

Yesterday's croissant is like an old girl friend, not much to look at and worse to spend time with. The bloom is both fragile and brief.

The schedule of our mornings, therefore, is governed by the time at which the day's fresh croissants can be gotten warm from the baker's oven. It may be that all Paris organizes itself around that moment, for hardly anyone goes to work before 9:30.

A Paris Notebook
C. W. Gusewelle
1985

Paris animals:

Although a taste for horse meat depends on habit or penury, the horse meat *"hippophagique"* appeals universally. Its golden heads rearing out of the bright red store fronts—sometimes two, sometimes a trio, with and without halos of golden horseshoes, inevitably evoke the frail petulant music of a far-distant carrousel.

The snail, too, sits well for its portrait; its big round coils of bright gold are one of the favorite emblems of the street of Les Halles. Butchers prettify calves' heads and pigs' heads with a sprig of flowers stuck in the ears or placed as rosettes on bovine foreheads. Less dead and yet not much alive, the burros and donkeys whose drooping heads and lank tails nod across the Concorde bridge, a set of magic-lantern silhouettes against the twilight, making their way home after a long day of pulling carts and children in the park.

Paris
Kate Simon
1967

COLOR

Long ago, walking the streets of Paris, studying the watercolors on exhibit in the shop windows, I was aware of the singular absence of what is known as Payne's gray. I mention it because Paris, as everyone knows, is pre-eminently a gray city. I mention it because, in the realm of watercolor, American painters use this made-to-order gray excessively and obsessively. In France the range of grays is seemingly infinite; here the very effect of gray is lost.

Quiet Days in Clichy
Henry Miller
1956

My father spent most of his time at the Meurice, so I walked the streets of Paris alone. For a week I seemed to carry a stone in my stomach, or in my throat, but I was too enchanted by the place to feel homesick for long—yet not quite at home in that extraordinary city. How different the facade here from Baltimore's scrubbed doorsteps, how different the anticipation of what will pass behind the facade.

It was a grey time, midwinter, and Paris is a grey city, the fortress color of metal and stone: a hard place that goes soft in a certain light. The light shifts, and with it the ambience. The sun may break through for no reason from a slit of unexpected heaven, a passing cloud will turn the gun-metal grey to pearl. A sense of elation might lie at the end of an obscure cul-de-sac, or, exploring a new quarter, my heart could shrink at the sudden onset of dark.

That first winter was dark, admittedly. (How much darker were the winters during the war?) Nevertheless a peculiar light filters through the dark, early and late. Paris will show herself when she chooses. There is a dark curtain one afternoon or evening; the curtain becomes a veil, the veil is drawn for an instant (a bearded man lifts his hat to a homely woman on the omnibus—why?) when the dark comes down? Or the grey sky will close in, with clouds low enough to touch, then lift lightly as a pigeon wings its way across the Seine.

Disappearances
WILLIAM WISER
1980

Love & Solace

IN PARIS ONE DOES NOT get sentimental before midnight.

Burning Houses
ANDREW HARVEY
1986

UNDER MIRABEAU BRIDGE FLOWS THE SEINE.
Why must I be reminded again
Of our love?
Doesn't happiness issue from pain?

Bring on the night, ring out the hour.
The days wear on but I endure.

Face to face, hand in hand, so
That beneath
The bridge our arms make, the slow
Wave of our looking can flow.

Then call the night, bell the day.
Time runs off, I must stay.

Le pont Mirabeau
GUILLAUME APOLLINAIRE
1913

My first day in Paris I walked
from Saint-Germain to the Pont Mirabeau
in soft amber light and leaves
and love was running out

For Poulenc
FRANK O'HARA
1963

Linda was rather annoyed. An Englishwoman abroad may be proud of her nationality and her virtue without wishing them to jump so conclusively to the eye.

"French ladies," he went on, "covered with the outward signs of wealth never sit crying on their suitcases at the Gare du Nord in the very early morning, while white slaves always have protectors, and it is only too clear that you are unprotected just now."

This sounded all right, and Linda was mollified.

"Now," he said, "I invite you to luncheon with me, but first you must have a bath and rest and a cold compress on your face."

He picked up her luggage and walked to a taxi.

"Get in, please."

Linda got in. She was far from certain that this was not the road to Buenos Aires, but something made her do as he said. Her powers of resistance were at an end, and she really saw no alternative.

"Hôtel Montalembert," he told the taxi man. "Rue du Bac. I apologize, madame, for not taking you to the Ritz, but I have a feeling for the Hôtel Montalembert just now, that it will suit your mood this morning."

Linda sat upright in her corner of the taxi, looking, she hoped, very prim. As she could not think of anything pertinent to say she remained silent.

Her companion hummed a little tune, and seemed vastly amused. When they arrived at the hotel, he took a room for her, told the liftman to show her to it, told the *concierge* to send her up a *café complet*, and kissed her hand, and said:

"Good-bye for the present—I will fetch you a little before one o'clock and we will go out to luncheon."

Linda had her bath and breakfast and got into bed. When the telephone bell rang she was so sound asleep that it was a struggle to wake up.

"A gentleman is waiting for you, Madame."

"Say I'm coming," said Linda, but it took her quite half an hour to get ready.

The Pursuit of Love
NANCY MITFORD
1949

I SHAVED AND CHANGED. In case it was all right for the Opéra. I was far too early, although I walked all the way to the Champs-Élysées. I sat down in a café next door, in a glassed-in veranda with infrared heating, and had hardly been served my pernod when the stranger with the pony-tail walked past, without seeing me, likewise far too early, I could have called her. . . .

She sat down in the café.

I was happy and drank my pernod without hurrying, I watched her through the glass of the veranda, she gave her order, then she waited, smoking, and once she looked at the clock. She was wearing her black duffel coat with the wooden toggles on cords and underneath it her blue evening dress, ready for the Opéra, a young lady trying out her lipstick. She was drinking a *citron pressé*. I was happier than I had ever been in Paris and I called the waiter so I could pay and go—across to the girl who was waiting for me! And yet I was quite glad that the waiter was so slow in coming: I could never be happier than at that moment.

Homo Faber
MAX FRISCH
1957

CHRISTMAS EVE IN PARIS. The day had been white and gray. They walked in Versailles this morning pitying the naked statues. The statues were glaring white. Their shadows were slate gray. The clipped hedges were as flat as their shadows. The wind was sharp and cold. Their feet were numb. Their footsteps made a sound as hollow as their hearts. They are married, but they are not friends.

Now it is night. Near Odéon. Near St-Sulpice. They walk up the Métro steps. There are the echoing sounds of frozen feet.

They are both American. He is tall and slim with a small head. He is oriental with shaggy black hair. She is blond and small and unhappy. She stumbles often. He never stumbles. He hates her for stumbling. Now we have told you everything. Except the story.

We look down from the very top of a spiral staircase in a Left Bank hotel as they climb to the fifth floor. She follows him around and around. We watch the tops of their heads bobbing upward. Then we see their faces. Her expression petulant and sad. His jaw set in a stubborn way. He keeps clearing his throat nervously.

They come to the fifth floor and find a room. He opens the door without any struggle. The room is a familiar seedy hotel room in Paris. Everything about it is musty. The chintz bedspread is faded. The carpet is ravelling in the corners. Behind a pasteboard partition are the sink and bidet. The windows probably look out on rooftops, but they are heavily draped with brown velour. It has begun to rain again and the rain can be heard tapping its faint Morse code on the terrace outside the windows.

She is remarking to herself how all the twenty-franc hotels in Paris have the same imaginary decorator. She cannot say this to him. He will think her spoiled. But she tells herself. She hates the narrow double bed which sags in the middle. She hates the bolster instead of the pillow. She hates the dust which flies into her nose when she lifts the bedspread. She hates Paris.

Fear of Flying
Erica Jong
1978

Every spring I fall in love with the same woman, and it happens the same way every time. After work at the typewriter, I take a walk in the sun, and there she is, as striking as ever, and there I am, struck dumb as Dante seeing Beatrice.

So Thackeray's hero fell in love at the Louvre with a woman standing there, silent and majestic, her hair light and her eyes gray, looking thirty-two but born 2000 years ago. Her name was Venus de Milo.

For me it is Paris.

The People of Paris
Joseph Barry
1966

I left the Guimet, walked to the Seine, threw my costly little pills into the river, and then walked and walked all around Paris. Charles, the joy of seeing Paris with that pall of self-hatred that I had been carrying round for years, utterly lifted! The relish of it! Walking down the rue Mouffetard, watching the old women selling peaches; sitting in the rue de Buci, watching the tourists watching the tourists; stumbling round the Jardin du Luxembourg, where even the worms wriggling on the flowerbeds were marvellously witty creatures. Some flowerpots high on a window-sill in the rue des Grands-Augustins seemed to me then the most beautiful things on earth. I often go to visit those flowerpots—no, I am not going to tell you the address . . . I walked and walked, and came at last to, of all places, the Shakespeare and Company Bookshop. I hadn't been there for years. It was nearly empty. The wiry old American who runs it was sitting by his desk reading. He didn't look up. It must have been two in the afternoon. I walked to the table in the middle of the shop where new books are displayed. Two caught my eye. The first was a large new illustrated edition of Blake's *Songs of Innocence and Songs of Experience.* I opened it with my eyes shut, praying for a sign. When I opened my eyes I read the lines,

> And we are put on earth a little space
>
> That we may learn to bear the beams of love.

Burning Houses
ANDREW HARVEY
1986

I WAS WALKING IN MONTMARTRE, and the steep tangle of its carnival streets, where few but seekers after the rawest pleasure ever came, seemed to promise an anonymity from which even the most painful memories might eventually ebb away. One could just take a room in one of those narrow, lobbyless, ten-francs-a-night hotels, wedged between a café and a *tabac,* and disappear. One could simply drop out of sight, and be living an entirely different life in an hour. The temptation of what Henry Miller had once called "quiet days in Clichy" tugged at me, because the mail that morning had been full of death back home.

A Wake in the Streets of Paris
JOHN CLELLON HOLMES
1987

DEAR SYLVIA:

Please tell me about Adrienne, if you feel you can. The *Souvenir* reached me here in the country day before yesterday, and in spite of all my shocks of the last six months, many losses by death of family and old friends, it was still a shock, there is no way without accepting without painful instinctive regret the death of anyone dear to us. Adrienne—you and Adrienne, for I thought of you together, even though you were both so distinct as individuals and friends in my mind—was a beautiful living being in my memory, though you were nearer to me; and I did have that pathetic fallacy of thinking of us all as immortal, or enough so for our purposes—we could never hear of each other's death!

How good of you to send me the *Souvenir*; I read in it, and a whole space of life comes back to me: that little pavilion and garden at 70 bis rue Notre-Dame-des-Champs, with you and Adrienne at dinner there, and such good talk! And your flat above 12 rue de l'Odéon, the parties there, the sparkle of life in *everybody* present, which you two could always bring out. And your wonderful books that I loved to roam around among, the best place I knew in Paris . . . Do you remember that dark rainy afternoon, almost evening, when Ernest Hemingway came in streaming rain from a big coat, you introduced us and then went to the back room to answer the telephone, and when you got back, Ernest was gone. He had just stood there looking across the big table at me with no particular expression on his face, I looked back, we never said one word to each other, and all at once he simply turned and bolted forth into the weather, and I have never seen him since. I am sure we have not been avoiding each other, it was just no doubt the right thing to happen. And Adrienne with her firmness and calmness and humorous wit, in her long gray beguine's dress and her clear eyes that could undoubtedly see through millstones, told such delicious things about her childhood. I remember best about how she and her sister Marie always wept when their parents took them to hear *Mélisande.* "From the first notes, we would begin to shed tears, and to sniff and sob, with people around us hissing at us for silence. We could not help it, and we wept just the same, every time. That music was *'si mystérieusement . . . émouvante!'"*

And now we shed tears for her, whose life was so mysteriously moving, its motives coming from such depths of feeling and intelligence they were hardly fathomable (except to you and to her nearest friends) but always to be believed in and loved: I knew well what she meant, I could guess the sources of her power. Bless her memory . . . Sylvia darling, the last time we saw each other was in the general confusion which seems always to attend my life in New York. I wish I could see you now, on this quiet hill in the country, all so tranquil and with time for everything. Or better in 12 rue de l'Odéon . . . but really, anywhere would do. Please let me know where you will be, what your plans are if you expect to change. With my same affection and remembrance and friendly love.

Katherine Anne

What was the date of her death?

From a letter sent to Sylvia Beach
KATHERINE ANNE PORTER
1956

DEAR M. MANZI,

Your funeral wreath arrived exactly as if to say your heart was with us during the sorrowful interval before the final separation from the only surviving of my two sons, a token as precious as it was ephemeral from both of you, because you are One with Joyant, united in the same tutelary sentiment towards him who was deprived of his just heritage, even if not on that account despairing.

These flowers from Paris deserved a more prompt expression of thanks. Flowers from Paris, I say, conquering flowers, it might be said, assuring artistic fame whatever form it may take among its many forms and revelations, displeasing perhaps the average idlers who may think that making money is all there is to an honest education.

Sincerity, it means everything.

They may criticize the brief works of the deceased, not old in years, but matured by so many trials, native to him and accidental as well.

He believed in his rough sketches, and you with him.

Thanks to your support he has been recognized and he owes it to you for having suppressed the malevolent opposition.

Joyant said to his schoolmate: He's a sensitive soul . . . to which a father may be permitted to add, an inoffensive one.

Between us there was never one of those flashes of feeling in which rancour replaces sweetness in the father-son relationship.

There you have the intimate side. He is your child for having fostered his art.

Lautrec

From a letter sent six days following the death of painter Henri Toulouse-Lautrec
COUNT ALPHONSE DE TOULOUSE-LAUTREC
1901

PARIS HISTORICAL

S ATURDAY, MIDNIGHT

I have reached this little hotel near the Gare du Montparnasse, and am thankful to have found a room.

From Vitré to Paris the train was no longer the ordinary Paris-Brest express. It was transformed into a military train, jammed full of men answering the call to arms. At every station, we were beseiged by crowds of reservists, until there was no more room and the engine could draw no more extra carriages. Then we crept slowly towards Paris, bearing our offering of human lives. One could feel, mingled with the effervescence, the excitement, the joy of approaching conflict, an undertone of anguish and sorrow, strikingly typified in that white-faced bride who in the course of the day's journey had seen her goal of happiness changed to an imprisonment of weary waiting in a strange city.

Paris Reborn
HERBERT ADAMS GIBBONS
1914

B UT THERE WAS ONE PHENOMENON we never had in the years 1918 to 1933 when I visited or lived in France, and that was a lost generation. Hemingway was responsible for this myth. In *The Sun Also Rises* he uses the epigraph: "'You are all a lost generation.'—Gertrude Stein in conversation" and it is now as impossible to rectify this fraud as it is to correct the false reports in history books of our time—the Damascus "massacre," for example.

The facts are simply:

1. Gertrude Stein was quoting someone.

2. The reference was to postwar workers, auto mechanics,
   and not to arts and letters.

As Miss Stein herself told it: when she complained to her garage owner about the bad job of repairing her auto, he replied that ever since the war he could no longer get skilled, responsible craftsmen of the good old days, and it was in this connection, and with no relation to the perhaps 100,000 artists, writers, expatriates crowding Paris, of which he probably knew nothing, that he remarked on a generation being lost.

Witness to a Century
GEORGE SELDES
1987

ANDRÉ DAVEN *(director of the Théâtre des Champs-Élysées):*

It was raining that morning in 1925. The Gare Saint-Lazare was teeming with its daily ration of pale, grim-faced commuters. Suddenly the bustling crowd froze. An excited, noisy, gaudy knot of people had just stepped off the Le Havre-Paris train. They were carrying strange-looking instruments and laughing uproariously. Their rainbow-colored skirts, fuchsia jeans and checked and polka-dot shirts lit up the gray platform. Unbelievable hats—cream-colored, orange, scarlet—dipped over their darting, laughing eyes. . . .

A tall, willowy girl in black-and-white-checked gardening overalls and an amazing hat detached herself from the group. "So this is Paris," she cried. These were Josephine's first words about the city she was to conquer.

Josephine
JOSEPHINE BAKER & JO BOUILLON
1977

FORTUNATELY FOR ME, a completely new type of American theatrical entertainment, with a new imported coloring, had just opened at the

Théâtre des Champs-Élysées. It was called *La Revue Nègre*. I wrote about it timidly, uncertainly, and like a dullard. As a matter of fact, it was so incomparably novel an element in French public pleasures that its star, hitherto unknown, named Josephine Baker, remains to me now like a still-fresh vision, sensual, exciting and isolated in my memory today, almost fifty years later. So here follows what I should have written then about her appearance, as a belated tribute.

She made her entry entirely nude except for a pink flamingo feather between her limbs; she was being carried upside down and doing the split on the shoulders of a black giant. Midstage he paused, and with his long fingers holding her basket-wise around the waist, swung her in a slow cartwheel to the stage floor, where she stood, like his magnificent discarded burden, in an instant of complete silence. She was an unforgettable female ebony statue. A scream of salutation spread through the theater. Whatever happened next was unimportant. The two specific elements had been established and were unforgettable— her magnificent dark body, a new model that to the French proved for the first time that black was beautiful, and the acute response of the white masculine public in the capital of hedonism of all Europe—Paris.

Paris Was Yesterday 1925–1939
JANET FLANNER
1972

THE SELECT, ON THE BOULEVARD MONTPARNASSE, was at that time a favorite gathering place for American newspapermen and not the notorious rendezvous it became later. For some weeks Isadora Duncan, now near the end of her tragic life, had been living in a cheap hotel in the rue Delambre, just around the corner from the Dôme. She had recently returned from a disastrous American tour in which she flaunted her Bolshevism on the stage.

The Young Intellectuals of Montparnasse, and of the Herald, had taken lately to gathering around Isadora as she held her court on the café terraces of the Quarter. She was poor now, but she was not dispirited. She was still a world-famous figure and she still had a great many admiring friends. Interested tourists also flocked around her table.

As the Sacco-Vanzetti case progressed, the scenes around Isadora became ever more stormy, and on this evening of the expected execution, she proclaimed loudly and violently on the Select terrace her opinions regarding the Massachusetts authorities.

Floyd Gibbons, a former hero-correspondent with a white patch over one eye shot out in the war, took issue with Isadora and led a counter-attack. He defended the honor of his country and the rightness of the executions even more loudly than Isadora had condemned them. Around him rallied the opposing forces, among them a couple of Herald men too. There followed one of the most violent scenes the Select, a particularly violent café, had ever witnessed. Passions ran high. Police from the rue Delambre station at length restored order.

Isadora, still believing that the executions would take place at midnight, which would be 5 A.M. Paris time, then marched through the rain to the American embassy, more than a mile away, and stood silently through the night before the portals, a burning taper in her hand.

Paris Herald
AL LANEY
1947

There was one event that foreshadowed the end, had we seen it for what it was. It occurred on the evening of August 23, 1927. We were living in Suresnes at the time, and, having put the baby to bed, my wife and I had gone down to the little river-front café that we frequented, for our coffee and *liqueur*. We found the place packed that night with workingmen whose eyes glared at us from all corners of the room. Not alone their eyes but their gestures as well were menacing. Riva and I had just remarked it when the proprietor, who knew us well, came up.

"If Monsieur-Madame will pardon me," he said, "I would suggest that they go. It is dangerous. You see, you are Americans, and—well, they do not like Americans—tonight."

We thought it strange; but as there was a stir at the near-by tables and, as I fancied, a movement in our direction, we decided to leave without asking any further questions.

"Well," I remarked, "I don't understand it, I'm sure; but seeing that we're out and this is the only decent place in Suresnes, why not go in to Paris—how about the Dôme? We haven't been there for a long while."

Coming down along the boulevard Raspail on the bus, we noticed signs of tumult as we neared the carrefour Vavin. There was a large crowd milling about in the square, and we could see residents of the Quarter, many of whom we recognized, running in all directions. As we alighted in front of the Rotonde and glanced down the boulevard du Montparnasse, we saw what was happening. We saw, but we did not understand. The café terraces were in turmoil; they were being invaded by men dressed like laborers, tables were being overturned, chairs were being hurled, there was a crash of china and glassware, and customers male and female were being tossed into the street. Someone ran past and shouted:

"Get out! Get out of here, quick!" We acted on this advice.

"What's it all about?" we wondered. First our experience at Suresnes, now this. Back in the place de l'Opéra once more, I decided to buy a paper and find out if I could. As I came up to the kiosk, my eye caught the headline: SACCO AND VANZETTI EXECUTED!

The Parisian workers were having their revenge.

Paris Was Our Mistress
SAMUEL PUTNAM
1947

M Y EARS, WHICH ARE UNUSUALLY KEEN, of a sudden picked out a delicate hum of lightest calibre away up in the clouds, which were now scudding across a misted moon . . . a small clear burring as of a toy, and then it was lost. . . . Suddenly, there was a silver flicker like the fin of a darting minnow out of one cloud into another.

"He's circling the field. *C'est lui!*"

"*C'est* Lindbergh!" the cries grew.

Suddenly, from the nearest cloud the bright wings flashed and veered downward, straight and sure to the waiting lane of flare-lit faces. He hit the runway precise and clean.

I heard a Frenchman say, "*Ce n'est pas un homme, c'est un oiseau.*"

Account of Lindbergh's landing at Le Bourget
CARESSE CROSBY
1927

TOWARDS THE MIDDLE OF MY LEAVE, I began to notice the large proportion of old and infirm people, and felt Paris as a bloodless town that some hemorrhage had drained of all its men. The sadness of the evenings, above all, affected me. Montmartre was dead and desolate. The Place St-Charles in the night's mirage struck me as having the gloomy vastness of some major road junction in the suburbs. Going down the Rue Pigalle I here and there perceived, like vitreous fissures, the dying gleam of the dance-halls through the curtains. I knew the jazz-spots had gone downhill, and these words of T.'s told me all that was needed about their death-throes: 'Let's not go to the Chantilly, it's too cold there.'

There was something more subtle in the air, moreover, which the Beaver made me feel very distinctly: it was a town of men without futures. 'A domestic existence,' she'd tell me. For what used to separate people entertainingly in peacetime was the fact that every man and every woman seemed like a door opened upon the outside, upon unknown futures. Each of them was waiting for something that I didn't know, and that depended partly on them; and it was that unknown future which cut them off from me, not the bus platform or patch of pavement which united us by contrast in the present. All that has disappeared. Most of the peoples I saw in the cafés, streets and dance-halls look very ordinary, don't talk about the war and occasionally even enjoy themselves. Yet I know their fate is settled, like that of the dead: they have nothing left to wait for but the end of the war—which does not depend on them. In the meantime, they occupy themselves as best they can; they let the war flow over them, arching their backs.

The War Diaries of Jean-Paul Sartre
JEAN-PAUL SARTRE
1940

Friday 14—First day of the Occupation. It is said that we must stay shut in for forty-eight hours.

With Sylvia observe from my windows the procession of motorcycles and trucks on the Boulevard Saint-Germain.

At noon begin to see people on the sidewalk.

In the afternoon, visit from Paul-Émile, who saw the procession of the first German battalions this morning at the Place de l'Étoile.

In the evening, great depression.

Saturday 15—Second day of the Occupation. We learn that we can go out from 7:00 in the morning to 9:00 in the evening, German time.

Morning: Halles. Sylvia came for me at 9:00. Nortier, Battendier, Varraz (wretched meat and fish). Sole.

Afternoon, went out with Rinette. Got meat at Adrien Brunel's. Deux-Magots, Flore, and Lipp shut. People's tension slackening: "What if the Germans are here, there will at least be order." It is said that they have supplied the evacuees with milk.

Monday 17—In the morning, went to the Samar., bought soap. Many German soldiers at the jewelry counter.

At twelve thirty, Pétain declaration. Sylvia lunches with me. Sirloin cold mayonnaise cauliflower.

Reopening of the bookshop (2:00 to 6:00). Saw three subscribers. Sold only one book: *Gone with the Wind*.

Saw Paul-Émile and Rinette. Paul-Émile gives the 11th arrondissement's impression of Russia. Many people wept listening to Pétain.

At 6:00 went out with Rinette, had tea at the Dôme; the Rotonde was reopened. Coming home, found nice tomatoes at the Russian restaurant. As I crossed the Luxembourg, the pink and red (?) flowers [crossed-out word] me; never saw so much variety in shades of pink.

Gloomy evening. I feel defeat and that it's going to be fascism.

The Very Rich Hours of Adrienne Monnier
ADRIENNE MONNIER
1940

HITLER ALSO TOOK BREKER ASIDE and began rhapsodizing on what they had seen the previous morning. "I love Paris—it has been a place of artistic importance since the nineteenth century—just as you do. And like you, I would have studied here if Fate had not pushed me into politics since my ambitions before the World War were in the field of art."

Adolf Hitler
JOHN TOLAND
1976

PEOPLE TALK ABOUT DEMARCATION LINES and food distribution; there is only one train a day from Cannes to Paris; I dine on four halves of sandwiches donated by four different friends. . . . Yes, it is war.

I live in the south of France now, and am in Paris on a visit. It's two years since I last saw the city. And how does it look after all this time? Paris looks as if it had fainted. You can hardly hear it breathe! The film has suddenly stopped . . . everybody is still in the same costume! The trees in the parks, the chestnuts and the birds, are they there to challenge the enemy? Only the Germans have cars. The avenues, the boulevards, the streets; they seem like immense empty race tracks an hour before the start of the first race.

The Germans talk about Paris as if it were a toy they had been given as a present. Bombs! Alarms! Misery! The drama keeps unfolding . . . dark, dooming, frightening, inexorcisable. Everywhere there is violence, ugliness . . . the smell of death.

Diary of a Century
Jacques-Henri Lartigue
1942

In truth, French cinema was extremely active during the war. The dance halls were closed, it was cold at home, people left the city only to look for food on the farms, and, at least where Paris was concerned, the movie theaters were never empty. Stairway windows had been daubed with laundry blueing, apartment windows had been blacked out, and a local volunteer known as a "sector warden" patrolled the streets to make sure that blackout regulations were being observed; if light trickled out of a window, he would blow a warning note on his whistle. No monument was illuminated, and especially not the Eiffel Tower. In short, the Germans and the Pétain government wanted to be sure that Paris could not be spotted from the air. This in no way prevented the English, in 1943, from bombing the La Chapelle quarter and especially the immense Dufayel warehouse on rue de Clignancourt, where I don't know what was stored. Paris could in truth no longer be called the City of Light; anybody who went out at night provided himself with a small flashlight that he would turn on when he left the Métro exit and keep on until he got home so as not to stumble along the sidewalk. As I remember it, the Sacha Guitry film *Donne-moi Tes Yeux* (!) is the only one to give a faithful idea of blackout reality.

As an example of the strictness with which blackout regulations were observed, I need only note that it was by no means rare to hear couples making love in the streets, standing in front of apartment house doors. Unfortunately, my young age at the time allows me to testify only to what I could hear.

André Bazin, the Occupation, and I
François Truffaut
1975

Somehow one gets the feeling, when looking at German newsreels, that there was a certain kind of openly racial propaganda which implied that the German talent for organization and discipline was required in order to bring about cleanliness and tidiness within the French confusion.

ELMAR MICHEL:

Yes, you are quite right. There was a propaganda department in Paris, but it was controlled from Berlin. May I point out that one of the first visits paid to me by the French government, at least on the ministerial level, was from the Minister of Communications in September of 1940. He came accompanied by the owner of a large racing stable, to ask me for authorization for the reopening of horse racing at Longchamps and Auteuil—since it served a real need of the people.

GERMAN NEWSREEL, *at the race track:*
Attendance at the races is better than ever before. No more doubt about it—Paris has found herself again!

ELMAR MICHEL:

I discussed the matter with my associates and we said: Why not? Horse racing started again, and there were races in Paris regularly until 1944.

NEWSREEL, *The Opéra in Paris—finale of an operetta, curtain, audience applauding.*

ELMAR MICHEL:

Thanks to us the theaters were also opened. They were very busy. You either went alone or with friends. Of course the Germans went to the races. And this is how the French and the Germans were able to meet; in fact, personal relations between different people on all sides could take place there, no doubt with differing motives.

You know of course that in France, post-war myths have led people to deny that any such personal contact ever took place.

ELMAR MICHEL:

Yes but they did.

The Sorrow and the Pity
MARCEL OPHULS
1969

PROBABLY ONE OF THE DULLEST stretches of prose in any man's library is the article on Paris in the Encyclopaedia Britannica. Yet when we heard the news of the liberation, being unable to think of anything else to do, we sat down and read it straight through from beginning to end. "Paris," we began, "capital of France and of the department of Seine, situated on the Ile de la Cité, the Ile St-Louis, and the Ile Louviers, in the Seine, as well as on both banks of the Seine, 233 miles from its mouth and 285 miles S.S.E. of London (by rail and steamer via Dover and Calais)." The words seemed like the beginning of a great poem. A feeling of simple awe overtook us as we slowly turned the page and settled down to a study of the city's weather graph and the view of the Seine looking east from Notre-Dame. "The rainfall is rather evenly distributed," continued the encyclopaedist. Evenly distributed, we thought to ourself, like the tears of those who love Paris.

Liberation of Paris
E. B. WHITE
1944

LIBERATION. PARIS IS OURS AGAIN! Everyone moves out on the streets to celebrate freedom. Flags wave everywhere. A holiday parade without a route . . . people move in every direction, pass each other, cross again, mix together, embrace, move to new groups. Some people are gay, others not at all. Even though my heart is happy, it is difficult to be aimless. I haven't been able to take any photographs for a long while. No film has been available. But I bring out an old roll of film I've been hoarding, hoping it is not too ancient to expose. The end of German occupation liberates my camera! I look out at Paris with new eyes. All of Paris! The miracle is not that she is only slightly scarred, nor that she has not been completely demolished, but that she is still *there.*

Diary of a Century
JACQUES-HENRI LARTIGUE
1944

A SHORT WHILE AFTER V. E. DAY, I spent a very happy evening with Camus, Chauffard, Loleh Bellon, Vitold, and a ravishing Portuguese girl named Viola. We left a bar in Montparnasse, which had just closed, and walked down to the Hôtel de la Louisiane; Loleh walked barefoot on the asphalt, saying: "It's my birthday, I'm twenty." We bought some bottles and drank them in the round room; the window was open to the warm air of the May night, and the people walking outside called out friendly words to us; for them, too, it was the first spring of peace. Paris was still as intimate as a village; I felt myself linked with all the unknown people who had shared my past, and who were as moved as I was by our deliverance.

Force of Circumstance
SIMONE DE BEAUVOIR
1963

Today's the day when the first batch of political deportees arrives from Weimar. They phone me from the center in the morning. They say I can come, the deportees won't be there till the afternoon. I go for the morning. I'll stay all day. I don't know where to go to bear myself.

Orsay. Outside the center, wives of prisoners of war congeal in a solid mass. White barriers separate them from the prisoners. "Do you have any news of so-and-so?" they shout. Every so often the soldiers stop; one or two answer. Some women are there at seven o'clock in the morning. Some stay till three in the morning and then come back again at seven. But there are some who stay right through the night, between three and seven. They're not allowed into the center. Lots of people who are not waiting for anyone come to the Gare d'Orsay, too, just to see the show, the arrival of the prisoners of war and how the women wait for them, and all the rest, to see what it's like; perhaps it will never happen again. You can tell the spectators from the others because they don't shout out, and they stand some way away from the crowds of women so as to see both the arrival of the prisoners and the way the women greet them. The prisoners arrive in an orderly manner. At night they come in big American trucks from which they emerge into the light. The women shriek and clap their hands. The prisoners stop, dazzled and taken aback. During the day the women shout as soon as they see the trucks turning off the Solférino Bridge. At night they shout when they slow down just before the center. They shout the names of German towns: "Noyeswarda?" "Kassel?" Or Stalag numbers: "VII A?" "III A Kommando?" The prisoners seem astonished. They've come straight from Le Bourget airport and Germany. Sometimes they answer, usually they don't quite understand what's expected of them, they smile, they turn and look at the Frenchwomen, the first they've seen since they got back.

The War
MARGUERITE DURAS
1985

SAL, DEAR:—

The trip here was like a kind of inconsequential taxi-ride by air. No depart, no sense of leave-taking, no sense of arrival. Much too soon Normandy is gone (with now and then a shell hole in the forest where it doesn't interfere) and suddenly one is in a bus passing old names like Avenue des Ternes. We waited for a taxi—tout mité [very run down]—which brought us to the Claridge 4 blocks away for 35 fr. (a newspaper costs 10 fr.). Claridge's is an ornate friendly caravanserai with corridors miles long, cavernous bathrooms, but with the wonderful flexible front the French always put on. There is no light in our arrondissement except from 7 p.m. to 11 p.m. daily & one shaves gropingly in dark bathrooms. Each arrondissement is deprived 3 days a week. They have really suffered but are still as eager, receptive, elastic, inventive, intelligent and gay. (The English admit they've lost something but are being sporting about it.) The French spirit is untouched, the English facade has been tarnished. Paris is strange tho. Touching, silent, pensive. Everyone scuttling about his business swiftly, deftly with none of the real free leisurely gayety of old. Values are so distorted that the purchase of an aperitif is no longer an idle gesture but takes on the mood of a major operation. You spend $30.00 in dollars (thousands in francs) and have no record of where or how or for what.

Yesterday was manufacturers all p.m. (we arrived 1 p.m.) dinner near the hotel, to-day mfrs. from 9 a.m. to 6. They're all so inventive, original, searching, impatient—and with no materials. The French genius is rising again. We're all half-alive compared to them,—and they have *nothing* to work with.

Mr. Schloss and his brothers send you their very best wishes and to Honoria too. I have a strange sense of stealing into a town I know and not making my presence known to it. To be here with strangers on a business mission is like a dream. Opposite is Fouquet's where one sat, the Pont Alexandre Trois, Larve, Langer,—one goes by them without comment to strangers. It's all very strange. Fortunately it never occurs to you to have time to ponder. Being one's age and wondering if it will ever return to itself gets all mixed up. There is no temptation to flâner [lounge], time, space and food are too uncertain and scarce.

Mme Hélène (or anyone) is out of the question. I regret. Not allowed to bring food into France, anyway. Will try to call Noel [Murphy]. Somehow I can't go into shops knowing that the French are not allowed to buy the stuff. All desire goes in the face of their real *need.* Their clothes, their thin bodies, and taut skins are moving beyond words.

To-morrow eve. at 8:50 we fly back. Sunday by motor to Walsall, mingham, Sheffield. Thursday, London again till Sun. then Dublin for 2 1/2 days.

Hope you're both keeping well and that E. & W. are a comfort. There are more dogs here than in Eng. I think they're really *fonder* of them. Lots of love to you both. I keep trying to think if you'd both enjoy Paris. In a way you somehow feel you shouldn't because they're all so worried. There's not much one can do to help. Yet the young are so much the same: loving couples, tête à têtes at tables in cafés, just as always. What a race! Love to you, my dears,—

From a letter sent to Sara Murphy
GERALD MURPHY
1947

D<small>EAR</small> S<small>AM</small>—

When I've finished sending things to Yale and done some typing and cleaned the flat and caught up with darning and patching—well then it will be spring and Basket and I will take walks and be in excellent form for when you do come. It's a nice quarter right across from the Pont-Neuf and four American blocks from Notre-Dame and just full of Gertrude. She used to wander all about it and at all hours—except the mornings before noon she never got out and so she always knew the leisurely afternoon life of the population when they could talk endlessly—which they and she did. When you come you'll like them better than ever you did because I think the liberation loosened them up beyond what they were when the Germans first came. There are lots of picture shows too more than there were. And the Petit Palais has all the treasures from all over France gathered together like the exposition of '36 and they say it may last for years. This is just the highlight because the Louvre won't be ready for years. It just has a few rooms opened.

From a letter sent to Samuel Steward
ALICE TOKLAS
1946

SINCE JULY 1954, Colette's life had been ebbing softly away. She slept for long hours, then would say a word or two, look at lithographic reproductions of some cherished exotic butterflies, and sink back into daydreaming. Her literary genius was akin to Matisse's artistic genius. She had given voice to the pulsing of the senses, to the instinctual forces governing nature, beasts, and humans, as he had redeemed condensed sensations in the visual arts.

At dusk on August 3, Colette regained consciousness for a moment. Her hands uplifted, her lips silently moving, she was probably back in the garden of her childhood, addressing Sido, her mother: "To attempt achievement is to come back to one's starting point. . . . My natural inclination tends toward the curve, the sphere, the circle."

The circle was complete; no more amorously selected words would align themselves on the pale blue paper under the light of the blue lamp. The eyes were closed; the hands fell back and were still. It was all over. Colette had expired, in her apartment overlooking the gardens of the Palais-Royal. The blue beacon that accompanied her laborious, sleepless vigils would no longer shine over Paris as a tutelary sign of life.

Matisse and Picasso
FRANÇOISE GILOT
1990

A DECEMBER NIGHT IN PARIS, frozen stars above a fretwork of Daumier chimneys. At the tip of the Ile, in the place where the morgue once was, the Crypt of the Deportees, with its portcullis of black blades, its two hundred thousand symbols representing the two hundred thousand missing, its earth from the camps and ashes from the crematoria, and its unknown corpse. In the little garden over which the shadowy bulk of Notre-Dame towers in vain (tonight, death is below ground), the delegations of survivors surround the tank which is about to bear the ashes of Jean Moulin to the Panthéon. The electric light will only be switched on again when the tank has left, escorted by five thousand young torch bearers sent by resistance organizations. The eye grows accustomed to the lunar haze: old comrades recognize one another. The ashes are brought in a child's coffin. The tank's engine starts up, and the torches manufactured today have the bluish quivering dazzle of acetylene lamps; feet still drag along in darkness, below heads which are brightly illuminated. Those who have just recognized one another, so like what they remembered in the moonlight (the torch bearers are their sons), discover that they nearly all have white hair.

Anti-Memoirs
ANDRÉ MALRAUX
1967

W ALK IN MORNING RAIN to Luxembourg Gardens, on an impulse I cannot define. To see uninjured trees? Gates are shut, chained, and padlocked. Behind them the silent trees. Walk all the way around, past the Senate, past the occupied Odéon—its curb a hedge of spilled garbage. This is the fringe of the battleground: more and more spilled *ordures*, a blackened car still running, another car looking as if it had been kicked and punched. Something dreamlike about the locked secret garden: green on green, chestnut petals all over the filthy pavement; behind the iron-spike fence a Sisley in the rain, a Corot with the sun gone.

Paris Notebooks
MAVIS GALLANT
1968

WHAT A WEEK PARIS HAS HAD with the students' riots, with a violence and sense of explosion that seized the whole city, for everyone knew what was transpiring, since everyone's sons or daughters were involved, or the neighbors! The violence and brutality of the police was not so astonishing as the fury of the students, amateurs in fighting in the streets and on the sidewalks. Had the young French fought like that against the young Germans in 1940, France would not have fallen in thirteen weeks, in weak disgrace.

From a letter sent to Natalia Danesi Murray
JANET FLANNER
1968

FRIDAY, MAY 8 (V-DAY)

Sign on door of bank, rue Littré: "Because of the Armistice" the bank is closed. There was no armistice in 1945. It was an unconditional surrender. No one remembers.

The Klaus Barbie trial begins on Monday.

French Journal
MAVIS GALLANT
1987

A City to Die In

So this is where people come to live; I would have thought it is a city to die in. I have been out. I saw: hospitals. I saw a man who staggered and fell. A crowd formed around him and I was spared the rest. I saw a pregnant woman. She was dragging herself heavily along a high, warm wall, and now and then reached out to touch it as if to convince herself that it was still there. Yes, it was still there. And behind it? I looked on my map: maison d'accouchement. Good. They will deliver her—they can do that. Farther along, on the rue Saint-Jacques, a large building with a dome. The map said: Val-de-grâce, hôpital militaire. I didn't really need to know that, but all right. The street began to give off smells from the sides. It smelled, as far as I could distinguish, of iodoform, the grease of pommes frites, fear. All cities smell in summer. Then I saw a house that was peculiarly blind, as if from a cataract; it wasn't on the map, but above the door there was an inscription, still fairly legible: Asile de nuit. Beside the entrance were the prices. I read them. It wasn't expensive.

And what else? A child in a baby-carriage standing on the sidewalk: it was fat, greenish, and had a clearly visible rash on its forehead. This was apparently healing and didn't hurt. The child was sleeping with its mouth open, breathing iodoform, pommes frites, fear. That is simply what happened. The main thing was, being alive. That was the main thing.

The Notebooks of Malte Laurids Brigge
Rainer Maria Rilke
1910

I attended early mass at the Sacré-Coeur church on January 1st, 1908. It was snowing lightly and very cold, and as I came away, at about eight, and descended the hill towards Paris, I was struck by the spectacle of the lame and the blind and miserable men and women who were appearing mysteriously from nowhere to descend the hill too, groping and hobbling down the slippery steepnesses. Such folk are an uncommon sight in Paris, where every one seems to be, if not robust, at any rate active and capable, and where, although it eminently belongs to the poor as much as to the rich, extreme poverty is rarely seen. In London, where the poor convey no possessive impression, but, except in their own quarters, suggest that they are here on sufferance, one sees much distress. In Paris none, except on this day, the first of the year—and on one or two others, such as July 14th—when beggars are allowed to ask alms in the streets. For the rest of the year they must hide their misery and their want, although I still tremble a little as I remember the importunities of the Montmartre cripple of ferocious aspect and no legs at all, fixed into a packing-case on wheels, who, having demanded alms in vain, hurls himself night after night along the pavement after the hard-hearted, urging his torso's chariot by powerful strokes of his huge hands on the pavement, as though he rowed against Leander, with such menacing fury that I for one have literally taken to my heels. He is the only beggar I recollect meeting except on the permitted days, and then Paris swarms with them.

A Wanderer in Paris
E. V. LUCAS
1909

ON A LONG TACK ACROSS THE ÉTOILE my gallant ship glides through the dusk . . . under full sail . . . she is heading straight for the Hôtel-Dieu . . . The whole town is on deck, still and calm. All those dead—I know them all . . . I even know the helmsman . . . He's my buddy . . . The pianist has caught on . . . He's playing the tune we need: "Black Joe" . . . for a cruise . . . to catch the wind and weather . . . and the lies . . . If I open the window, it will be cold . . . Tomorrow I'm going to kill Monsieur Bizonde, who keeps us going . . . the trussmaker, in his shop . . . I want him to travel he never goes out . . . My vessel groans and pitches over the Parc Monceau . . . She's slower than last night . . . She's going to hit the statues . . . Two ghosts go ashore at the Comédie-Française . . . Three enormous waves carry off the arcades of the rue de Rivoli. The siren screams against my windowpanes . . . I close my door . . . A roar of wind . . . My mother appears with her eyes popping out . . . She scolds me. Misbehaving as usual. Vitruve comes running . . . More good advice. I rebel . . . I give them hell . . . My fair ship is limping. Those females can wreck the infinite . . . She's off course, it's shameful . . . Nevertheless she heels over to port . . . there's no more graceful craft afloat . . . My heart follows her . . . Those bitches would do better to run after the rats that are fouling the rigging . . . She'll never make that tack with her ropes so taut . . . got to slacken them . . . let out three turns before the Samaritaine! I shout all that out over the rooftops . . . My room is going to sink. I've paid for it, haven't I? Every last cent. With my lousy rotten existence.

Death on the Installment Plan
LOUIS-FERDINAND CÉLINE
1952

I N THE LOWER DEPTHS of the Paris underworld, streets are so narrow that dwellers can lean out their windows and shake hands with people in houses across the way. In daylight these streets are ill smelling, moldy-looking, and dung-colored, but night transforms the drab walls with an all-over cloak of charcoal and silver, the same lovely satin that is draped on Notre-Dame, on the

Chamber of Deputies, and the buildings facing the Place de la Concorde. Close to you, the walls of houses are brushed with melancholy hues, and street lamps throw disks of soft light on sidewalks and gild the contours of the buildings.

Everything is filled with ache and misery. As the people of this district have their own language, a tough, simile-filled slang, so they have their own music. It is in the mood of the place, as melancholy as the color; the nasal whining of concertinas comes from small bars, called *bals*, meaning ballrooms. (The French have a compulsion to name things delicately: a brassiere is called a throat supporter; a procurer is called a stand-by.)

Before going to the *bas-fonds* the visitor should be told that this form of sightseeing costs dearly in disillusionment; the misery is genuine, the women leaning against the wall or tapping their heels along the pavements, fiercely protecting their assigned stretch of sidewalk, are neither daughters of joy, temple dancers of fiction, nor the mascaraed houris of the Arab Paradise. With the rarest exceptions, they are gross, pitiful creatures, homogeneous to their surroundings.

The Paris Underworld
Ludwig Bemelmans
1955

FIRST PERSON SINGULAR

PARIS IS THE ONLY PLACE I SAW at that time that had stallions on the streets instead of geldings, and women going through the streets without hats. The women were free, feminine. The men, very male, all going about their work. All simple, alive. Each one arranging his wares with love, with a sense of order, with gaiety.

The 'good' Americans who were so good at home were charmed by the so-called naughtiness and beauty of Paris when they came with their money. They paid to have the songs, the freedom, the atmosphere, reproduced for them in cafés, and then slowly the French, through their natural desire to get money, destroyed their own freedom to be natural, finally giving the impression of unnaturalness.

From a letter sent to Hamilton Easter Field
ALFRED STIEGLITZ
1920

POUR ME DISTRAIRE organized a fiacre race. Four partners in four fiacres? A prize of five hundred francs. Down the Champs-Élysées bound for the Ritz-Bar, about a mile in all. At the Concorde the four hacks were well grouped and it was not until after the Rue de Rivoli that Joan and I were defeated in the final sprint by half a length, the others trailing behind. Brandy for the coachmen, cocktails for ourselves, and a brimming bowl of champagne for the broken-down Marguerite. To make of life a race; to "run the straight race through the Sun's good grace."

Shadows of the Sun
HARRY CROSBY
1922

THAT VERY EARLY MORNING (two or three o'clock, it must have been) Eugène Jolas took me to the Bal Nègre to meet Caresse and Harry Crosby . . . we eventually found them on the perilously high and crowded balcony of the nightclub that had become the current rage (it being the thing to have two or three negro friends, provided they were in the jazz scene) . . . Caresse and Harry were drinking champagne, talking, laughing . . . looking down on the chaos of the dance arena below . . . The Bal Nègre, near dawn, the wildly stepping dancers with no more than an inch between the coupled men and women . . . are as vividly alive today as a Lautrec canvas; the saxophone wails louder and louder, the beat of the drums is almost deafening. In the white blaze of the lights . . . I see the features of Caresse's face, her bronze hair cut in a bang across her forehead, and Harry's face, already then committed to the look of the skull he paid daily and nightly homage to in the rue de Lille.

The Crosbys: An Afterword
KAY BOYLE
1928

So WE CAME TO THE RITZ HOTEL and the Ritz Hotel is devine. Because when a girl can sit in a delightful bar and have delicious champagne cocktails and look at all the important French people in Paris, I think it is devine. I mean when a girl can sit there and look at the Dolly sisters and Pearl White and Maybelle Gilman Corey, and Mrs. Nash, it is beyond worlds. Because when a girl looks at Mrs. Nash and realizes what Mrs. Nash has got out of gentlemen, it really makes a girl hold her breath.

And when a girl walks around and reads all of the signs with all of the famous historical names it really makes you hold your breath. Because when

Dorothy and I went on a walk, we only walked a few blocks but only in a few blocks we read all of the famous historical names, like Coty and Cartier and I knew we were seeing something educational at last and our whole trip was not a failure. I mean I really try to make Dorothy get educated and have reverence. So when we stood at the corner of a place called the Place Vendôme, if you turn your back on a monument they have in the middle and look up, you can see none other than Coty's sign. So I said to Dorothy, does it not really give you a thrill to realize that that is the historical spot where Mr. Coty makes all the perfume? So that when Dorothy said that she supposed Mr. Coty came to Paris and he smelled Paris and he realized that something had to be done. So Dorothy will really never have any reverance.

Gentlemen Prefer Blondes
ANITA LOOS
1925

THE DEUX-MONDES IN PARIS ended about a blue abysmal court outside our window. We bathed our daughter in the bidet by mistake and she drank the gin fizz thinking it was lemonade and ruined the luncheon table next day.

The hotel in Paris was triangular-shaped and faced the St-Germain-des-Prés. On Sundays we sat at the Deux-Magots and watched the people, devout as an opera chorus, enter the old doors, or else watched the French read newspapers. There were long conversations about the ballet over sauerkraut in Lipps, and blank recuperative hours over books and prints in the dank Allée Bonaparte.

Zelda Fitzgerald: The Collected Writings
ZELDA FITZGERALD
1924/1927

IT SEEMED QUITE NATURAL then that hot afternoon to stroll across the large half-moon of the fine old parade-grounds that face the monumental facade of the Ducal Palace, then to step up to the rows of *fiacres* that still waited there always for passengers. I had never ridden in one, although only two or three nights before I had listened to the clear sounds of a couple of them clip-clopping along the quay underneath our windows in Paris, and I had recognized their sound without question as part of the reality of the dream I was to live in from then on.

Long Ago in France
M. F. K. FISHER
1991

WHEN I ARRIVED IN PARIS, I had no idea where to stay, so I headed for the Hôtel Ronceray in the passage Jouffroy, where my parents had spent their honeymoon in 1899 and where, incidentally, I'd been conceived. Three days later, I found out that Unamuno was in Paris; it seemed that some French intellectuals had outfitted a boat and gone to rescue him from his exile in the Canary Islands. He participated in a daily peña at La Rotonde in Montparnasse, where I met my first *métèques*, those "half-breed foreigners" the French right wing was always vilifying for cluttering up the sidewalks of Paris cafés. I went to La Rotonde almost every day, the way I used to go to cafés in Madrid, and sometimes I'd walk Unamuno back to his apartment near the Étoile, a distance that gave us a good two hours' worth of conversation.

My Last Sigh
LUIS BUÑUEL
1982

Dᴜʀɪɴɢ ᴛʜᴇ ᴅᴀʏ I ʜᴀᴅ ᴛᴇʟᴇᴘʜᴏɴᴇᴅ Gertrude Stein. It was Sunday, her at-home evening. I told her about Abdelkader, and she said to bring him along. We were let in by a maid, who opened the salon door for us. The room was full of people; Gertrude Stein stood in the middle of it, talking. Suddenly she gave one of her hearty, infectious laughs and slapped her thigh, as she was wont to do in such moments. "*C'est elle?*" said Abdelkader in a stage whisper, wide-eyed. "*Mais c'est un homme, ça!*" I hushed him and we went in.

Without Stopping
Pᴀᴜʟ Bᴏᴡʟᴇꜱ
1972

Tᴏɴɪɢʜᴛ, ᴀꜱ I ʟᴇꜰᴛ ᴛʜᴇ ʀᴇꜱᴛᴀᴜʀᴀɴᴛ, I passed by Notre-Dame and stopped at a pissoir to take a leak. I was torn by conflicting impulses—one, to circle Notre-Dame and soak it up; two, to tear off a poster in the pissoir which interested me exceedingly. All over Paris now there are advertisements (London likewise) put out by the municipality, warning the public against contracting venereal infections. And are they realistic? Are they grim? Wait till I get one for you, showing the various stages of syphilis or gonorrhea (from the germ plasm up to the death skull—a leering, grinning figure of death and disease with empty sockets).

Letters to Emil
Hᴇɴʀʏ Mɪʟʟᴇʀ
1930

Iɴ 1934, ᴀᴛ ʜɪꜱ ꜰʟᴀᴛ in the Rue du Vieux-Colombier, Paul Valéry and I once happened to be discussing Gide: "Why," I asked him, "if you're indifferent to his work, do you rate his *Conversation with a German* so highly?" "What's that?" he asked. I reminded him. "Ah, yes! It must be because it has a beautiful example of the imperfect subjunctive." Then, with the relative seriousness he was wont to mix with his patrician slang: "I'm fond of Gide, but how can a man allow young people to be the judges of what he thinks? And anyway, I'm interested in lucidity, not sincerity. Besides, nobody gives a damn." Thus did he often dismiss ideas which, in Wilde's phrase, he regarded as the stuff of drawing-room conversation.

Anti-Memoirs
ANDRÉ MALRAUX
1967

LAST NIGHT I WAS ABOUT TO GO UP TO BED when the bell rang. It was Proust's chauffeur, Céleste's husband, bringing back the copy of *Corydon* that I lent to Proust on 13 May and offering to take me back with him, for Proust is somewhat better and sends a message that he can receive me if it is not inconvenient for me to come. His sentence is much longer and more complicated than I am quoting it; I imagine he learned it on the way, for when I interrupted him at first, he began it all over again and recited it in one breath. Céleste, likewise, when she opened the door to me the other evening, after having expressed Proust's regret at not being able to receive me, added: "Monsieur begs Monsieur Gide to have no doubt that he is thinking constantly of him." (I noted the sentence right away.)

Journals of André Gide
ANDRÉ GIDE
1921

I REMEMBER AS AN EXCEPTIONAL OCCASION—for Proust never went out except at night—Proust calling for me up in the rue d'Anjou one *morning,* in the Albaret fiacre, to go see the Mantegna *Saint Sébastien* at the Louvre. He had the look of an electric light bulb left on during the day—or of a telephone ringing in any empty apartment. In the Louvre, people no longer looked at the pictures, but at him, with astonishment.

Past Tense
JEAN COCTEAU
1952

A WEEK LATER IN PARIS IT WAS BASTILLE DAY, Aaron had gone to London, and I sat on the *terrasse* of the Dôme. Some friends walked up, bringing with them a fantastic girl in a very small bathing suit. Apart from being beautiful, she looked as though she had come off the beach at Juan-les-Pins. Which, she explained charmingly, was exactly what she had done. In a fit of pique she had got onto the *Train Bleu* just like that, with no clothes and no luggage. And there was no way of buying anything for another three days because it was the *Quatorze Juillet.* What was she going to do? She shrugged, and we laughed. It soon became necessary to do something, however, inasmuch as the waiter arrived before long to say that the *patron* could not permit nudity on the *terrasse* of the Dôme. We were ordering plenty of drinks, the *soucoupes* were piling up, and we felt moved to protest. The *patron* sensibly suggested that we sit downstairs in the *sous-sol.* Jacqueline thought it a perfect solution; she had had enough of being stared at. We continued to drink in a corner of the basement near the *W. C. pour Dames.*

Without Stopping
PAUL BOWLES
1972

M Y FRIEND THE PAINTER Georges Mathieu presented me with
a very precious fifteenth-century arquebus whose breech was inlaid with ivory.
And on the 6th of November, 1956, surrounded by a hundred sheep sacrificed in
a holocaust to the unique first copy on parchment, I fired, on board a barge in
the Seine, the first lead bullet filled with lithographic ink in the world. The
shattered bullet opened the age of "bulletism." On the stone, a divine blotch
appeared, a sort of angelic wing whose aerial details and dynamic strength surpassed all techniques employed up to this day. In the week that followed I gave
myself up to new and fantastic experiments. In Montmartre, in front of a deliri-
ous crowd, surrounded by eighty girls on the verge of ecstasy, I filled two
hollowed-out rhinoceros horns with bread crumbs soaked in ink, and then
calling upon the memory of my William Tell, I smashed them on the stone. A
miracle for which God should be thanked: the rhinoceros horns had drawn the
two open arms of a windmill. Then a double miracle: when I received the first
proofs, a bad printing had left spots on them. I believed it to be my duty to
incorporate and accentuate these spots in order to illustrate paranoiacally the
whole electric mystery of the liturgy of the scene. Don Quixote encountered
externally the paranoiac giants he carried within himself.

Diary of a Genius
SALVADOR DALÍ
1964

M Y SCHOOLROOM DAYS CAME TO AN END, and Idden and I
were sent to Paris to stay with a French lady and perfect our knowledge of
French at the Sorbonne.

My mother came with us to help us get settled. Always deeply suspicious of the French, she was in a furious rage against the whole nation from the

moment of our arrival at the Gare du Nord, where our porter bravely tried to fight her down about the amount of his tip. My mother stood her ground, and much to the amusement of Idden and myself the porter went off grumbling in French, "You're the kind of Englishwoman who murdered Joan of Arc."

Daughters and Rebels
Jessica Mitford
1960

DID YOU EVER SEE Frémiet's equestrian statue of Joan of Arc in Paris? If so, you remember the fine figure of Joan, erect, her chest sticking out. Jeanne Valérie Laneau posed for that statue at the age of 14, sixty-two years ago. Yesterday, aged 76, she died in Paris, and strangely, like Joan of Arc, she died in fire, burned by an exploding oil heater. The original Joan died on a blazing bonfire, poor reward for saving her king and France.

Anonymous

HOW ARE THE BEDBUGS at the Récamier this year?" she asked. "Are they all gone?"

"Every last one of them as far as my room is concerned," I chuckled. "The people over there are always very nice to me, probably because you and I are friends and you and Gertrude first sent me there. They always give a room with a view of the square."

"And the bells of St-Sulpice bounce you out of bed every Sunday."

"At least three feet," I laughed.

From a conversation with Alice Toklas
Samuel M. Steward
1977

IN THE PALAIS-ROYAL
is a garden
planted with mostly white:
Beauty enough
to make men wise.

You took me there
remember,
at the hour
when day and night change hands:
we saw their fingers mingle.

And it surprised us both
I think,
that knowing and feeling all we cannot know
could enter us like scent
and linger there,
and leave again,
night falling around us.

And so we will go again
to Paris
and again,
to stand knee-deep
in gardenia and nicotiana and Colette:
Two friends,
faithful,
waiting.

In the Palais-Royal
GREGORY RILEY
1992

A SILVERY JUNE AFTERNOON. A June afternoon in Paris twenty-three years ago. And I am standing in the courtyard of the Palais-Royal scanning its tall windows and wondering which of them belong to the apartment of Colette, the *Grand Mademoiselle* of French letters. And I keep consulting my watch, for at four o'clock I have an appointment with this legendary artist, an invitation to tea obligingly obtained for me by Jean Cocteau after I had told him, with youthful maladroitness, that Colette was the only living French writer I entirely respected—and *that* included Gide, Genet, Camus, and Montherlant, not to mention M. Cocteau. Certainly, without the generous intervention of the latter, I would never have been invited to meet the great woman, for I was merely a young American writer who had published a single book, *Other Voices, Other Rooms*, of which she had never heard at all.

Now it was four o'clock and I hastened to present myself, for I'd been told not to be late, and not to stay long as my hostess was an elderly partial invalid who seldom left her bed.

She received me in her bedroom. I was astonished. Because she looked precisely as Colette ought to have looked. And that was astonishing indeed. Reddish, frizzly, rather African-looking hair; slanting, alley-cat eyes rimmed with kohl; a finely made face flexible as water . . . rouged cheeks . . . lips thin and tense as wire but painted a really brazen hussy scarlet.

And the room reflected the cloistered luxury of her worldlier work— say, *Chéri* and *The Last of Chéri*. Velvet curtains were drawn against the June light. One was aware of silken walls. Of warm, rosy light filtering out of lamps draped with pale, rosy scarves. A perfume—some combination of roses and oranges and limes and musk—hovered in the air like a mist, a haze.

So there she lay, propped up by layers of lace-edged pillows, her eyes liquid with life, with kindness, with malice. A cat of peculiar gray was stretched across her legs, rather like an additional comforter.

But the most stunning display in the room was neither the cat nor its mistress. Shyness, nerves, I don't know what it was, but after the first quick study I couldn't really look at Colette, and was somewhat tongue-tied to boot. Instead, I concentrated on what seemed to me a magical exhibition, some fragment of a dream. It was a collection of antique crystal paperweights.

There were perhaps a hundred of them covering two tables situated on either side of the bed: crystal spheres imprisoning green lizards, salamanders, *millefiori* bouquets, dragonflies, a basket of pears, butterflies alighted on a frond of fern, swirls of pink and white and blue and white, shimmering like fireworks, cobras coiled to strike, pretty little arrangements of pansies, magnificent poinsettias.

At last Madame Colette said, "Ah, I see my snowflakes interest you?"

The White Rose
TRUMAN CAPOTE
1970

M Y VISIT TO COCTEAU—to "The inspired Jean," as Paul Goodman calls him—was paid Friday at eleven in the morning. A perfect, sunny day. I was in a state of terror which wouldn't have taken hold if I had just been going to see him cold. But I'd written him a warning of my approach in two flirtatious letters (snapshots of myself enclosed), and received eloquent and equally flirtatious replies.

He lives at 35 rue Montpensier in a smallish and very low-ceilinged apartment overlooking the Palais-Royal garden, the hordes of playing children, and the Véfour restaurant. (He can wave to Colette who lives on the same courtyard, but he spends most of his days now with his friend—Paul, from the film of *Les Enfants Terribles*—in the country at Milly; he can work nowhere else.)

He opened the door himself, and immediately showed me into a tiny room at the right where he followed, locking the door, after telling the maid not to bother us for two hours. This tiny room had a tiny bed with a scarlet spread piled high with books, prints, current art and literary magazines, none of the pages of which was cut, a desk and a drafting table (each also piled high with books), a telegraph set (out of order), and a blackboard reaching to the ceiling, on which was a chalk drawing by Jean of a boy's profile, a Siamese cat (female) . . . . Cocteau himself wore a floor-length sky-blue dressing gown cut like a medieval priest's; the sleeves completely covered his hands, though his gestures were so violent that I caught frequent glimpses of the longest fingers I have ever seen. His voice had no relation to the one we've heard at the movies: it sounded rather higher; he talked incessantly. He didn't sit down once, but continually paced the little room, occasionally petting the cat in passing. His favorite words are *con* and *emmerder;* and he scarcely makes a sentence without one or the other. Yet everything about the congested atmosphere was elegance itself; none of those crumbling corners one finds in even the grandest French homes.

The Paris & New York Diaries of Ned Rorem
NED ROREM
1951

I AM MOVING. I am rapturously pleased. I cannot get the room I have retained at the Hôtel Continental till November 17. Tiny, in the roof, with a glorious view all over the horizon of Paris and the Tuileries gardens beneath, oh what a pleasure to have a vista of beauty; room newly painted, milk white, lovely new cherry-colored carpet, small elderly bathroom, only one big closet, two corner placards [armoires] with rounded mirrors (rounded at top, Gothic fashion), sloping roof, the whole utterly picturesque, with a tiny balcony of zinc, a railing of narrow iron bars which must date from the Second Empire in style and with the mansard roof bulging up at either side. I fancy I could perhaps squeeze a deck chair there if I kept my knees under my chin. The price is slightly less than the Scribe, but I shall be paying about $125 monthly for a room, roof, a bath—but with beauty.

From a letter sent to Natalia Danesi Murray
JANET FLANNER
1949

THIS MORNING I AWOKE VERY EARLY. Across the empty rue de Rivoli the birds sang wildly in the lush trees. I waited as long as I could, but was almost surely the first one to ring for breakfast (I am reading a good Simenon-non-Maigret: l'homme du petit chien).

I drank half the coffee and milk *hot.* Delicious. Then I ate most of a croissant and a roll, all the butter, most of the strawberry jam. Then I finished the coffee and milk—almost too cool, but bitter and good. (The bread, like that at [Café de] la Paix, was disappointing. Of course yesterday was Sunday.) The butter was sweet and pale, in a little foil thing, as was the jam. Ho hum for the old sticky messy unsanitary *pots* . . . I felt fine.

This morning I made motions toward my employers. Nobody was there. Finally Mme Dupont was. She sounds nice—quite efficient for a change. I was to call at 2:30ish.

I went out and walked great distances—really not more than about two miles probably, but getting used to traffic, and going in little shops, and crawling over street repairs . . . I bought some bath oil, eau de cologne, and soap!!! Worth's *Je Reviens.* I would *never* do such a self-indulgent thing if I weren't alone. I bought six oeillets, yellow and red, and two bunches of a clear light yellow flower that looks like a little thistle blossom. They are lovely in the room. I got this cahier, air paper, pencils, and so on.

When I came back, Janet Flanner had called. She called again. I went up to her room, above mine. She has just moved here permanently. It is exactly like mine but perhaps four feet more shallow, being higher in the mansard. It made me dream again of coming here when I am old.

She is effusive, amusing, kind and cold. I like her very much, and am attracted to her sureness of power.

Paris Journal
M. F. K. FISHER
1966

A NEGRO TAXI DRIVER, exceptionally courteous for the Paris of 1950, says to me as we pass in front of the Comédie-Française surrounded by cars: "The House of Molière is full tonight."

Notebooks 1942–1951
ALBERT CAMUS
1950

PARIS LOVED *Porgy & Bess.* We were originally supposed to stay at the Théâtre Wagram for three weeks, but were held over for months. After the first week I discovered that I couldn't afford to stay in the hotel that had been assigned to me. The policy of the company was to pay singers half their salary in the currency of the country we were in and the other half in dollars. I sent my dollars home to pay for Clyde's keep and to assuage my guilt at being away from him.

I moved into a small pension near Place des Ternes, which provided Continental breakfast with my tiny room. There was a cot-sized bed and just space for me and my suitcase. The family who owned the place and my fellow roomers spoke no English, so perforce my French improved.

One evening after the theater a group of Black American entertainers who lived in Paris came backstage. They enchanted me with their airs and accents. Their sentences were mixed with Yeah Man's and Oo la la's. They fluttered their hands and raised their eyebrows in typically Gallic fashion, but walked swinging their shoulders like Saturday-night people at a party in Harlem.

Bernard Hassel, a tall nut-brown dancer, worked at the Folies-Bergères, and Nancy Holloway, whose prettiness brought to mind a young untroubled Billie Holliday, sang at the Colisée. Bernard invited me to see the night life of Paris.

"Alors, something groovy, you know?"

We went to the Left Bank, and he showed me where F. Scott Fitzgerald and Hemingway did some flamboyant talking and serious drinking. The bareness of the bar surprised me. I expected a more luxurious room with swatches of velvet, deep and comfortable chairs and at least a doorman. The café's wide windows were bare of curtains and the floor uncarpeted. It could have been a Coffee Shop in San Francisco's North Beach. High up over the facade hung a canvas awning on which was stenciled the romantic name DEUX-MAGOTS.

L'Abbaye was a bar owned by Gordon Heath, a Black American who provided his own entertainment. He sang in a weak but compelling voice and

projected an air of mystery. After each song the audience showed their appreci-
ation by snapping their fingers. Heath did not allow hand-clapping.

Singing' and Swingin' and Gettin' Merry Like Christmas
MAYA ANGELOU
1976

FOR YEARS JAMES BALDWIN CAME TO PETER'S twice a week
for dinner in Paris because Baldwin was starving . . . now he makes about one
million a year (and is not really a very good writer tho he is indeed in the headlines, even here, daily) . . . Poor Jimmy (they call him) . . . and yet, such luck,
to be negro at the right time. We stayed late, drinking bottles of IMPORTED (15
cents a bottle) french wine.

From a letter sent to her family
ANNE SEXTON
1963

I MET GIOVANNI DURING MY SECOND YEAR IN PARIS, when
I had no money. On the morning of the evening that we met I had been turned
out of my room. I did not owe an awful lot of money, only around six thousand
francs, but Parisian hotel-keepers have a way of smelling poverty and then they
do what anybody does who is aware of a bad smell; they throw whatever stinks
outside.

Giovanni's Room
JAMES BALDWIN
1969

WE TOOK THE MÉTRO TO PIGALLE and got out in the hot sun
by the honky-tonk square and began climbing the little narrow roads to the

top of Montmartre; the shops were dark and stenchful holes and reeked of garlic and cheap tobacco. In the sun there was a magic of decay: scabbed pastel posters, leprous umber walls, flowers sprouting out of filth. Climbed rue Vieuville & series of steeply angled steps to Place du Tertre, which was chock full of tourists and bad bad artists in various stances doing charcoal portraits or muddy paintings until a small man asked if he could cut my silhouette *"comme un cadeau,"* so I stood in the middle of the square in the middle of Montmartre and gazed at the brilliant restaurants in the middle of a gathering crowd which ohed and ahed and which was just what the little man wanted—to attract customers.

The Journals of Sylvia Plath
SYLVIA PLATH
1956

EDMUND WHITE walks us over to the Orangerie des Tuilleries after lunch and we see Monet's *Water Lilies.* I remember seeing them from my time before in Paris in 1968. The idea of Monet's *growing* the flowers he would later paint—very lovely. Idea of painting the unseen because he was painting light in water. The way an approximation becomes all one needs of the real at certain times.

Paris Journal
TESS GALLAGHER
1987

TWO AND A HALF YEARS LATER, Billy Graham came to Paris proper and held his press conference in the Palais d'Orsay Hôtel. The time, this time, was the Birmingham crisis—and Billy proffered as his civil rights solution "supernatural love." On the Sunday following, he opened his eight-day rally in a tent for 10,000 pitched in the Paris Flea Market.

At 8 p.m. the tent—"specially built in Germany for this crusade," said the press handout—was a third full, mostly, it seemed, of middle-aged women. Never has a French audience looked so American. Except for the gypsies, who were there by the hundreds, attracted, I first thought, by the giant tent and the intriguing possibility of having *their* fortunes told.

On the platform was the promised choir of 300 women, in white blouses, rehearsing Negro spirituals in French under the direction of Reverend Cliff Barrows, "Melody Lane, Greenville, S.C." The choristers were as bespectacled as the audience. Are Protestants more bespectacled than Catholics because of too much Bible reading?

People drifted in as the flea marketeers went home, but the back benches remained empty. The front benches were reserved for *conseillers*, except for one place occupied by a rather wonderful *clochard* who rose solemnly and drunkenly to his feet to pronounce *"bravo"* twice after a hymn sung by George Beverly Shea, "America's beloved gospel singer," thus sorely trying the saintly patience of the old woman sitting next to him.

At 8:35 there was a minute of silent prayer. At 8:36 the choir sang *"Jésus est le chemin."* At 8:40 there was a collection to the sound of an organ played *sotto voce* by Donald Paul Hustad, "born: Sioux Agency, near Echo, Yellow Medicine Co., Minn."

At 9, Billy Graham was introduced. At 9:05 he began to speak, in short bursts of his instant religion, packaged, he indicated, in the economy-size Bible held in his hand. And each burst was instantly translated by the same small French pastor, echoing the trumpet of Billy's voice, duplicating in miniature his every gesture.

It was cool and the audience was cold. The fastest tongue of the West faltered, but not for long. "The world cries freedom! [tr.] Freedom! [tr.]

Freedom! [tr.]," he trumpeted. "Social freedom [tr.], political freedom [tr.], sexual freedom!" And the Frenchman fumbled with "sexual," translating at first as "intellectual."

Jazz-quick, Billy improvised scornfully on the pessimism of Sartre and Camus, Einstein and the Buddha, but only the French pastor, not his French audience, was interested in this refutation of intellectuality.

The People of Paris
JOSEPH BARRY
1966

I DON'T KNOW WHERE YOU ARE NOW, VICTORIA.
They say you have children, a trailer
in the snow near our town,
and the husband you found as a girl
returned from the Far East broken
cursing holy blood at the table
where nightly a pile of white shavings
is paid from the edge of his knife.

If you read this poem, write to me.
I have been to Paris since we parted.

As Children Together
CAROLYN FORCHÉ
1981

VINCENT VAN GOGH PAINTED A YOUNG MAN with the stem of a cornflower between his teeth. I know of no face nearer to Sartre's than that. It is the generosity of a newly ploughed field, Sartre's face.

That day he said: "You ought to work up the section about the epilep-tic in the park." I would have liked to, but it was beyond me.

His voice transfigures him. When I listen to him, I understand just how far the timbre of our voices betrays and informs against us. Sartre speaks, and first and foremost his voice is irrefutable. Sartre speaks, and it is so dense yet so airy between the words. It's more than melodious: it is percussive. In twenty-two years, Sartre has talked to me for a maximum of ten minutes. The second time, after having laid his paper down in the same way on his table in the Deux-Magots, he said to me: ". . . The titles of Hegel's chapters are more tiring than the text . . ." I have never got over that.

Mad in Pursuit
VIOLETTE LEDUC
1970

IN PARIS, I THOUGHT I HAD FOUND everything, particularly the skills of the craft.

My Life
MARC CHAGALL
1931

A FINAL REMINDER. Wherever you are in Paris at twilight in the early summer, return to the Seine and watch the evening sky close slowly on a last strand of daylight fading quietly, like a sigh.

Paris
KATE SIMON
1967

CREDITS

Below each entry is the original text in which the entry appeared, the author's name, and the date the entry was written. The credits that follow here appear in the same order as the entries and acknowledge the source from which copyright permission was obtained.

CONDITIONS OF ITS GREATNESS

Excerpt from "Bypassing Rue Descartes" © 1988 by Czeslaw Milosz Royalties, Inc. From *The Collected Poems, 1931–1987* by Czeslaw Milosz, published by The Ecco Press. Reprinted by permission. ✦ *Paris Reborn* by Herbert Adams Gibbons, published 1915 by The Century Co. ✦ From *Keeping a Rendezvous* copyright © 1991 by John Berger. Reprinted with permission of the author. ✦ Excerpt from "May, 1932" in *The Diary of Anaïs Nin, Volume I, 1931–1934*, copyright © 1966 by Anaïs Nin, reprinted with permission of Harcourt Brace & Company. ✦ From *Letters of Thomas Mann, 1889–1955* by Thomas Mann, translation by Richard & Clara Winston. Copyright © 1970 by Alfred A. Knopf, Inc. Reprinted by permission of the publisher. ✦ Excerpt from "Paris, Capital of the Nineteenth Century" in *Reflections: Essays, Aphorisms, Autobiographical Writings* by Walter Benjamin, translated by Edmund Jephcott and Peter Demetz, English Translation copyright © 1978 by Harcourt Brace & Company, reprinted by permission of the publisher. ✦ *Paris and Environs* published by Grieben's Guide Books, Vol. 214 - 1929. ✦ "A Wake in the Streets of Paris" from *Displaced Person* copyright © 1987 by John Clellon Holmes. Reprinted with permission of The University of Arkansas Press. ✦ Excerpt from a letter "To Robert McAlmon, May 2, 1921" in *The Letters of T. S. Eliot, Volume I, 1898–1922* by T. S. Eliot, copyright © 1989 by SET Copyrights Limited, reprinted by permission of Harcourt Brace & Company and Faber and Faber Ltd. ✦ From *The Locked Room* copyright © 1986 by Paul Auster. Reprinted with permission of Paul Auster. ✦ *Autobiography of an Ex-Coloured Man* by James Weldon Johnson, published 1927. ✦ From *Voices in the Mirror* copyright © 1990 by Gordon Parks. Reprinted with permission of Doubleday, a division of Bantam, Doubleday, Dell Publishing Group, Inc.

PARISIANS

MEANS OF TRANSPORT

permission of Pantheon Books, a division of Random House, Inc. ✚ From *A Paris Notebook* copyright © 1985 by C. W. Gusewelle. Reprinted with permission of the author.

Color

Love & Solace

INDEX OF AUTHORS & PLACES

Allée Bonaparte, 133

Allée des Reines, *12, 14*

Angelou, Maya, 145–147

Anonymous, 139

Apollinaire, Guillaume, 18, 91

Arc de Triomphe, 3, 20, 41, 72

Auster, Paul, 8

Auteuil, 113

Avenue Daumesnil, 42

Avenue des Ternes, 18, 117

Baker, Josephine, 104, 105

Bal Nègre, 132

Baldwin, James, 37, 147

Barnes, Djuna, 15–16

Barry, Joseph, 38, 95, 148–150

Barthes, Roland, 21–22

Beach, Sylvia, 81–82, 97, 98, 110

Beaubourg Palace, 26

Bel-Air, 44

Bemelmans, Ludwig, 30, 127–128

Benjamin, Walter, 5–6

Berberova, Nina, 20, 71–72

Berger, John, 4

Bernstein, Richard, 36–37

Bishop, Elizabeth, 68–69

Bois de Boulogne, 14, 42

Botzaris, 44

Bouillon, Jo, 104

Boulevard Diderot, 42

Boulevard Montparnasse, 23, 105, 107

Boulevard Pasteur, 71

Boulevard Raspail, 61, 107

Boulevard St-Germain, 16, 19, 110

Boulevard St-Michel, 17, 51

Bowles, Jane, 69–70

Bowles, Paul, 70, 135, 137

Boyle, Kay, 132

Brassaï, 47–49, 52–55

Brasserie Lipp, 110, 133

Bryson, Bill, 41, 47

Buñuel, Luis, 134

Café Costes, *130*

Café Cyrano, 67

Café de Flore, 110

Café de la Paix, 26, 144

Campo-Formio, 44

Camus, Albert, 73, 115, 141, 145

Cannes, 111

Capote, Truman, 141–142

Carrefour Vavin, 107

Carrousel, 50

Cartier, 133

Céline, Louis-Ferdinand, 20, 126–127

Chagall, Marc, 21, 151

Chamber of Deputies, 128

Champs-Élysées, 3, 8, 20, 25, 71, 73, 93, 131

Chantilly, 109

Chartier, 67

Clichy, 97

Cocteau, Jean, 137, 141, 142, 143

Colette, 50, 120, 140, 141, 142, 143
Colisée, 146
Comédie-Française, 35, 51, 70, 127, 145
Conciergerie, 42
Connolly, Cyril, 70–71
Coty, 133
Crimée, 44
Croix-de-Chavaux, 44
Crosby, Caresse, 108, 132
Crosby, Harry, 131, 132
Crypt of the Deportees, 120
Culbertson, Judi, 29
Dalí, Salvador, 138
Danube, 44
de Beauvoir, Simone, 115–116
de Bremond d'Ars, Yvonne, 65
de Toulouse-Lautrec, Count Alphonse, 99
Debussy, Claude, 14
Delacroix's Studio, 19
Deligny, 58
Deux-Magots, 110, 133, 146, 151
Deux-Mondes, 133
Dôme, 105, 107, 110, 137
Ducal Palace, 134
Duras, Marguerite, 35–36, 116–117
École des Beaux-Arts, 16, 17, 18
École Normale, 56
Eiffel Tower, 21, 22, 49, 51, 112
Eliot, T. S., 7, 19
Esplanade of the Louvre, 79
Étoile, 68, 72, 126, 134
Faubourg St-Germain, 19
Fauchon, 57
Faulkner, William, 82
Filles du Calvaire, 44

Fini, Léonor, 27–28
Fisher, M. F. K., 134, 144–145
Fitzgerald, F. Scott, 36, 146
Fitzgerald, Zelda, 133
Flanner, Janet, 104–105, 122, 143–144, 145
Flea Market, 148
Folies-Bergères, 146
Forché, Carolyn, 150
Fouquet's, 118
Frisch, Max, 93–94
Galerie Vivienne, 32
Gallagher, Tess, 148
Gallant, Mavis, 18–19, 121, 122
Gare d'Orsay, 116
Gare du Montparnasse, 103
Gare du Nord, 92, 139
Gare St-Lazare, 8, 104
Gary, Romain, 79–80
Gibbons, Herbert Adams, 3–4, 103
Gide, André, 136, 141
Gilot, Françoise, 120
Gordon, Alastair, 21
Grand Véfour, 143
Green, Julian, 19, 26, 55
Grieben's Guide Book, 6
Guimet, 95
Gusewelle, C. W., 44, 83
Gysin, Brion, 23
Harvey, Andrew, 73, 91, 95–96
Hass, Robert, 58–59
Hemingway, Ernest, 38, 55, 80–81, 103, 146
Holmes, John Clellon, 6–7, 49–50, 96–97
Hôtel Claridge, 117
Hôtel Continental, 8, 143

Hôtel de la Louisiane, 115
Hôtel des Trois Moineaux, 22
Hôtel du Bosphore, 72
Hôtel du Quai Voltaire, 66
Hôtel Meurice, 87
Hôtel Montalembert, 92
Hôtel Récamier, 15, 52, 139
Hôtel Ritz, 5, 92, 132
Hôtel Ronceray, 134
Hôtel Scribe, 144
Hôtel Washington, 25
Hôtel-Dieu, 48, 126
I. M. Pei's Pyramid, 21, 46
Ile de la Cité, 13, 42, 47, 49, 114, 120
Ile Louvier, 114
Ile St-Louis, 3, 47, 114
Institut de France, 13, 18
Jardin des Plantes, 42
Jasmin, 44
Johnson, James Weldon, 8–9
Jong, Erica, 94–95
Juan-les-Pins, 137
Just, Ward, 20
Kafka, Franz, 42–43
Kerouac, Jack, 26–27
Kinnell, Galway, 74
Kramer, Jane, 33
Kuh, Patric, 57–58
L'Abbaye, 146
La Chapelle, 112
La Madeleine, 26, 57
La Rotonde, 23, 107, 110, 134
Laney, Al, 105–106
Lartigue, Jacques-Henri, 111–112, 115
Le Bourget, 108, 117
Le Procope, 51

Le Vésinet, 41
Leduc, Violette, 73, 150–151
Les Halles, 83, 110
Les Invalides, 74
Levin, Harry, 56–57
Liebling, A. J., 16–17, 29, 81
Longchamps, 113
Loos, Anita, 132–133
Louvre, 13, 17, 21, 42, 46, 47, 50, 95, 119, 137
Lucas, E. V., 125–126
Luxembourg Gardens, 12, 14, 16, 73, 80, 96, 110, 121
Luxembourg Museum, 81
Malraux, André, 120–121, 135–136
Mann, Thomas, 5
Mansfield, Katherine, 67–68
Matthiessen, Peter, 17–18
Maugham, W. Somerset, 71
Maxim, 38
McCarthy, Mary, 38, 60
Métro, 42, 43, 44, 56, 60, 67, 80, 94, 112, 147
Métro Abbesses, 40
Métro Lecourbe, 80
Métro Stalingrad, 2
Miller, Henry, 19, 53, 54, 87, 135
Milly, 143
Milosz, Czeslaw, 3
Mitford, Nancy, 29–30, 92–93
Mitford, Jessica, 138–139
Monnier, Adrienne, 97, 98, 110–111
Mont-St-Michel, 70
Montmartre, 43, 66, 86, 96, 109, 126, 138, 148
Montparnasse, 16, 38, 106, 115, 134

Moore, Judith, 55–56
Morand, Paul, 14–15
Morris Columns, 53
Murphy, Gerald, 117–119
Musée d'Orsay, 90
Nabokov, Vladimir, 24–25
Napoléon's Tomb, 29
Neuilly, 54
Nin, Anaïs, 4
Notre-Dame, 3, 5, 42, 47, 48, 49, 51, 65,
    70, 115, 119, 120, 127, 135
O'Hara, Frank, 92
Odéon, 94, 121
Opéra, 26, 27, 43, 93, 114
Ophuls, Marcel, 113–114
Orangerie, 148
Orwell, George, 22
Osborne, Lawrence, 43–44
Ourcq, 44
Palace of the Senate, 15
Palais d'Orsay Hotel, 148
Palais-Royal, *front cover*, 50, 120, 140,
    141, 142
Panthéon, 56, 121
Parc Monceau, 127
Parks, Gordon, 9
Passage des Beresinas, 20
Passage Jouffroy, 134
Passage Véro-Dodat, 78
Petit Palais, 119
Petit Trianon, *102*
Pigalle, 147
Place de l'Étoile, 110
Place de l'Observatoire, 81
Place de l'Opéra, 108
Place de la Concorde, 3, 8, 20, 72, 128, 131

Place de la Contrescarpe, 80
Place des Ternes, 146
Place des Vosges, 55
Place du Palais-Bourbon, 41
Place du Tertre, 148
Place St-Charles, 109
Place St-Sulpice, 52
Place Vendôme, 20, 133
Plath, Sylvia, 147–148
Pont Alexandre III, 3, 118
Pont d'Austerlitz, 42
Pont d'Iéna, 73
Pont de l'Archevêché, 3
Pont de la Concorde, 83
Pont de Solférino, 117
Pont de Sully, 47
Pont de Suresnes, 41
Pont des Arts, 13
Pont Mirabeau, 91, 92
Pont-Neuf, 13, 119
Porte Dauphine, 43
Porte Dorée, 42
Porter, Katherine Anne, 81, 97–98
Préfecture de Police, 48
Pritchett, V. S., 13
Putnam, Samuel, 107–108
Pyramides, 44
Quartier latin, 48, 57
Queneau, Raymond, 65
Randall, Tom, 29
Renoir, Jean, 79
Restaurant des Beaux-Arts, 16
Rhys, Jean, 16, 23–24, 67, 72
Riley, Gregory, 140
Rilke, Rainer Maria, 14, 36, 58, 59–60, 125
Ritz-Bar, 131

Root, Waverley, 50–51
Rorem, Ned, 66–67, 142–143
Rue Abbé-de-l'Epée, 53
Rue Aumont-Thieville, 18
Rue Bonaparte, 15, 16, 17
Rue d'Anjou, 137
Rue d'Argenteuil, 79
Rue de Babylone, 20
Rue de Beaune, 71
Rue de Bourgogne, 54, 71
Rue de Buci, 17, 96
Rue de Castiglione, 20, 58
Rue de Clignancourt, 112
Rue de Fleurus, 61
Rue de Grenelle, 16
Rue de l'Ancienne-Comédie, 51
Rue de l'Arrivée, 24
Rue de l'École de Medecine, 17
Rue de l'Odéon, 97, 98
Rue de l'Université, 71
Rue de Rivoli, 8, 20, 58, 127, 131, 144
Rue de Seine, 17
Rue de Vaugirard, 16, 81
Rue Delambre, 105, 106
Rue des Écouffes, 57
Rue des Grands-Augustins, 18, 96
Rue Descartes, 3
Rue du Bac, 92
Rue du Cloître-Notre-Dame, 48
Rue du Pot-de-Fer, 56
Rue du Vieux-Colombier, 135
Rue Jacob, 71
Rue Lecourbe, 80
Rue Lhomond, 57
Rue Littré, 122
Rue Montpensier, 142

Rue Mouffetard, 56, 96
Rue Notre-Dame-des-Champs, 81, 97
Rue Pigalle, 109
Rue Royale, 57
Rue St-André-des-Arts, 17
Rue St-Jacques, 53, 125
Rue St-Supplice [Rue St-Sulpice], 24
Rue Vieuville, 148
Rue Watt, 124
Rueil, 41
Sacré-Coeur, 5, 66, 125
Samaritaine, 110, 127
Sartre, Jean-Paul, 55, 75, 109, 150, 151
Seine, 3, 5, 13, 18, 42, 47, 49, 50, 51, 65, 70,
    79, 88, 95, 114, 115, 138, 151
Seldes, George, 103–104
Select, 106
Sexton, Anne, 147
Shakespeare and Company Bookshop, 96
Simon, Kate, 33–35, 83, 151
Société Générale, 27, 28
Sorbonne, 5, 15, 17, 48, 138
Square du Furstemberg, 19
St-Cloud, 41
St-Germain, 41, 42
St-Germain-des-Prés, 51, 133
St-Sulpice, 52, 94, 139
St-Julien-le-Pauvre, 18
Ste-Chapelle, 42
Ste-Elisabeth, 18
Stein, Gertrude, 60–61, 103, 104, 119, 135,
    139
Steward, Samuel, 119, 139
Stieglitz, Alfred, 131
Stock Exchange, 20
Styron, William, 25

Suresnes, 107, 108

Théâtre des Champs-Élysées, 104, 105

Théâtre Wagram, 145

Three Musketeers Café, 75, 82

Toklas, Alice, 119, 139

Toland, John, 111

Tour St-Jacques, 13, 48

Truffaut, François, 112–113

Tuileries Gardens, 20, 26, 50, 57, 64, 72,
 79, 143, 148

Tuileries Palace, 79

Val-de-grâce, 125

Versailles, *ii*, 41, 94

Victor Hugo Museum, 55

Vincennes, 42

Vitré, 103

Wallace Fountains, 53

Wharton, Edith, 41–42, 71

White, Edmund, 70

White, E. B., 114–115

Williams, William Carlos, 74–75

Wiser, William, 87–88

Wright, James, 52, 66

Zanzi-Bar, 23

Zweig, Paul, 57